Poppy's Path to Love

Great Smoky Mountain Getaways

Elsie Davis

Sweet Romance Publishing

*To all my readers, thanks for the blessing
you give with your kind words, love, and support.*

Jeremiah 29:11
*"For I know the plans I have for you," declares the LORD,
"plans to prosper you and not to harm you, plans to give
you hope and a future."*

<h1 style="text-align:center;">Chapter One</h1>

❤

"Next stop, Lincoln, NC." The train conductor's voice crackled over the loudspeaker announcing their destination, something Poppy had heard for the last fifteen stops and two days of traveling. It would have been better if she had paid for a club car and been able to sleep more comfortably. But she had chosen to pocket the extra train fair Mr. Jordan Perry, her new employer, had sent her for the ticket, preferring to use it for her additional traveling expenses and putting the rest into her dwindling savings account.

The trip was over, and her nerves kicked into an almost uncontrollable agitated mode of anticipation. When Poppy first discovered the ad for a nanny, she had been leery of applying. But after the second Sunday of the people at church giving her the cold shoulder, not to mention, some of her co-workers at Brighton Elementary holding secret whisper sessions and pointing in her direction, she had had enough. People in town would not want her teaching their young children once Rupert Harris's lies about her made the rounds.

Her ex-boyfriend had certainly done a number on Poppy and her reputation. She too had been blinded by his exterior attitude of love and kindness, and it was only recently she had seen the level of his deception. Not that anyone would believe her if she tried to bring light to the truth. Rupert was the golden boy of Whittling, New York, star quarterback, and the deacon's son. He could do no wrong.

This is why Poppy had to leave town.

It had come as a shock when a quick response to her application had come back with a job offer. As Mr. Perry's new nanny to his five-year-old daughter and his housekeeper, the perk of living in his home was something she could not pass up. A sure sign, this was the next step in her life.

Perhaps the town of Lincoln would even be the place she had dreamed of finding since turning eighteen and forging her own way in the world—a place where she belonged. A place to call home.

The train brakes screeched to a stop, the sound reminding her of fingernails scratching down a chalkboard. Poppy stood and gathered her backpack and carry bag, moving toward the exit. The door opened and she stepped down, holding the rail for support. Stepping out onto the platform she looked around, but the place was like a ghost town with only a few people walking about. Nothing like the hustle and bustle of the Whittling train station.

A uniformed man stepped off the train and opened a compartment, withdrawing her two suitcases and depositing them next to her. "Have a good day, ma'am," he said with a nod.

"Thank you." Poppy handed him a tip and he turned, stepped back into the train, disappearing as the doors closed. Mr. Perry had mentioned he would send someone to collect her, and she assumed the person would be here, sign in hand, alerting Poppy to his identity.

One lone man stood off to the side. Several times he glanced in her direction, but he made no move toward Poppy, his glance dismissive rather than welcoming. Definitely not her ride to the Perry farm. Everyone else paid her no attention at all.

Poppy sat down to wait. Perhaps Mr. Perry had forgotten her arrival, or he'd gotten the times mixed up. In which case, she would need to make her own arrangements to get to his place. Having long since learned to take care of herself, being resourceful came automatically. Thirty minutes was all she would give the man to make an appearance before she took matters into her own hands.

Fifteen minutes later, another train arrived, its loud whistle and obnoxious brakes proceeding the billowing cloud of smoke from the steam engine. One by one, passengers got off and greeted their waiting party, exchanging hugs and smiles. Others got on the train.

Only one person remained as the train departed five minutes later. The same man who had shot her a dismissive look earlier. Dressed in jeans, a flannel shirt, and a Stetson hat hung low on his forehead, he was a handsome man; his athletic build and well-worn boots a sure sign he was not a city cowboy. He glanced at her once again and Poppy looked away.

Poppy warred within herself as to whether to approach the man or not, but he shook his head and turned away again, but not before glancing at his watch. Surely, if he were here to collect her, he would have simply asked. It was time to be bold and time to leave the train station. At the very least, the man was a local and might be able to direct her to the Perry farm.

"Excuse me, sir," she said, taking a few steps in his direction.

The closer she got, the more aware she became of his rugged good looks, and the more nervous it made her.

His lips formed a tight line of tension, her intrusion into his personal space clearly an irritation.

She searched her brain for the right words. "My ride hasn't shown up and I was wondering if you could direct me to the Perry farm?"

One eyebrow shot up as his brow furrowed before the man shook his head. "The Perry farm? What business do you have there?"

It was not like she had to explain herself to a stranger. How hard was it to answer a simple question? "I think that's my concern. Do you know the way or not?" It was her turn to push back. After a long ride in an uncomfortable seat on the train, her patience level was not at its best.

"I do. In fact, I'm Jordan Perry, and I'm waiting to pick up someone who hasn't bothered to turn up as scheduled. Goes to show you age doesn't always come with a guarantee of efficient responsibility. State your business now, as it'll save you a trip to my farm."

Her brain was still stuck on the fact the man in front of her was Jordan Perry—her new boss. But something was wrong; his words trickled in; the meaning unclear. "I'm not sure what you mean about age and efficiency, but I'm Poppy Delacorte, the woman you hired as a live-in nanny and house-keeper." She shifted the backpack onto her suitcase, tired of holding it.

"There must be some mistake. You can't possibly be Poppy Delacorte." He scowled; the firm set of his jaw revealing his rejection of the truth.

Poppy had to laugh. The man's expression was priceless, his eyes clouded with confusion. "But I am. I would think I know my own name."

"Then who's this?" He pulled a paper out from his back pocket, unfolded it, and held it up for her perusal. "This is the woman I'm supposed to meet—a much older Poppy Delacorte as you can tell."

"I have no idea who that woman is, but I'm Poppy, trust me." She was not sure how the mix-up occurred, but the fact remained he'd hired her for the job, and it was high time they headed for his place. Poppy was tired and wanted to get cleaned up.

"This can't be right, and it won't work. You're too young for the job. I would have never hired you. Did you switch the photos or something?" he asked, his hardened gaze disconcerting.

"I did nothing of the sort." Poppy huffed, not liking his attitude. "What do you have against my age? You do realize that would be age discrimination."

"Lady, I don't care what you want to call it, but there's no way you can move into my own and take care of my daughter. It's out of the question." He crossed his arms in front of his chest, his feet wide in a stance of defiance.

Poppy's gaze grew blurry as she realized what he was really saying. The man was serious—he did not want her services. Did not want her in his home. Lincoln was quickly shaping up to be her shortest stay in a town, not her new home. "What do you expect me to do? I just got here and have nowhere to stay."

"You should have thought of that before you attached a fake photo to your application," Jordan ground out.

The man was quickly turning into a bore—no, make that a bear. "For the last time, I didn't. Maybe the agency made a mistake, but the resume I attached to the application is my own. My qualifications stand, as does my willingness to take the job. You sounded desperate to have someone step in quickly. What's changed?" She had to convince him to let her stay.

"You changed." He scowled. "You're too young."

"What do you have against a younger adult handling the job you posted?"

"I wanted someone old. Someone like this," he said, holding up the paper and pointing to it. "The last nanny ran off to get married. Before that, it was woman after woman dropping in with offers to help, hoping to become the next Mrs. Perry and unabashedly using my daughter to make it happen. I won't tolerate the same nonsense, which is why I wanted someone older. Someone past all using feminine wiles and a façade to catch a husband. Instead, I get you."

Poppy winced. It was not of her doing, but it did not change the result. She had been fired before her first day. "I get it, and I'm sorry." She looked away, dumping her bag on the ground next to suitcases, and sat down on the taller one. It was everything she had in the world, having long since learned to travel light as she moved from town to town. Five times in nine years. Correction, make that six. She had come here with the intention of staying and was already having to ride out of town.

The question was, however, where would she go?

Mr. Perry stepped closer, the scuffed-up toes of his boots mere inches from hers. "Here." He reached into his back pocket and pulled out his wallet. "Take this money for your return trip. It should more than cover your return ticket home and there's some extra for your trouble."

Poppy would have liked to toss the money back at him, but it would be foolish. And it was the least he could do considering the circumstances. She had to think of it more like a blessing, God looking out for her. "Thanks," she mumbled, folding the wad of cash in half, and shoved it in her purse without looking or counting it. It did not matter how much; it would not make up for another round of smashed dreams.

Mr. Perry did not realize there was no home to go back to—by choice. Poppy found it easier to pack up and move when things got difficult and the idea of being tied to one place had no appeal. As a drifter moving from town to town, each new city offered her the hope of a brighter tomorrow.

Until then, she never wanted to feel trapped.

Chapter Two

♥

MR. PERRY TURNED AND walked away, leaving Poppy in turmoil as she tried to decide what to do next. A ticket out Lincoln was her top priority, and then she would have to find a place to stay for the night. But where to go? Lugging her suitcases with the extra bags stacked on top, she pulled them toward the lobby of the train station. After two attempts to get through the door with her luggage, she gave up, sitting down on one of them and unable to hold her frustration in check, broke into tears.

There was no one else here and she was tempted to leave a suitcase outside and manage them one at a time. In the city, it was the surest way to lose half of what you owned. And for Poppy, that did not amount to much so she could ill afford to lose it.

Her stomach rumbled, reminding her she had not eaten anything other than the granola bars and snacks she'd tossed in her purse for the trip. The thought of another chocolate-covered peanut bar did not excite her as much as the lure of a juicy hamburger with a pile of fries to satisfy her food cravings.

Poppy stood; decision made. Food first, lodging second, and a ticket out of Lincoln after she was settled in someone for the night. It would give her the time she needed to figure out where to go next.

She dragged her cases, stopping frequently to adjust the falling bags attached to the handles, and made her way down Main Street. A blinking café sign announced she had arrived at Cotswold Café and she stopped. The same problem existed in getting inside the building, but at least here, there were cars and people and not a lonely platform, bereft of people and the perfect target location for someone to rob her.

Reluctantly, she let go of one case, hauling the other one up the two steps and through the front door, stopping at the table closest to the front window to deposit her things. She quickly headed back out the door and reached for her suitcase just as someone else did.

"Let go, that's—" she started to say, yanking the suitcase toward her and glancing up at the man trying to steal it.

Jordan Perry. The last person she expected to see.

"I know. I'm trying to help you." His deep, gravelly voice cut through her tension as she wrapped her brain around his words.

"Oh. But why?" she asked, scrunching her face up to pin him with a hard look, refusing to let go of her suitcase.

"I've changed my mind. Well, at least in part. I need you. I mean I need your services."

Poppy shook her head, unsure what to make of his explanation. "I still don't understand, Mr. Perry. Fifteen minutes ago, you fired me, so start talking. And let go of my suitcase." She huffed.

He did as she asked and let go. "Jordan. The name's Jordan, and like I said, I've changed my mind. I want to hire you, temporarily anyway, if you're okay with my conditions, that is." He removed his Stetson and rubbed a hand through his wavy, brown hair as if it pained him to have to admit he needed her. Well, he did not need to worry—she did not need him or his job offer with conditions.

"I'm not interested. Good day, *Jordan*." She pulled her case up the two steps, leaving him staring at her open-mouthed. The man must not get told no very often, which made her answer seem all that much better.

"But you haven't heard my offer," he insisted, taking the stairs and pulling the door open to allow her to pass through, following her inside.

Poppy did not have any pressing agenda, other than to eat. Common sense won out. Besides, part of her was more than a little curious about the offer. "Fine. Buy my lunch and you can talk, but I'm not promising anything."

Jordan nodded, sitting down at the table with her. "I can do that." The worried frown on his face touched a soft spot in her heart. The man exuded confidence and strength and yet he was worried about something.

The server came over and took their orders, filled their water glasses, and left. An awkward silence ensued.

"Let's hear it," she prompted. Poppy was stuck having lunch with him now, but it did not mean she had forever.

"So, here's the deal." Jordan let out a deep breath. "I already told you why I couldn't have you working for me and living in my home. But the truth is, right after I left you, I called the woman who's been helping me out until, well, you, arrived. I asked her to stay later today and for the next few days while I tried to figure something else out. Unfortunately, she's leaving in the morning for Colorado. Her daughter's expecting a baby any day and she plans to be there."

"And what does this have to do with me?" Poppy asked. "I arrived and you fired me. End of story."

"Except, I've got no one to watch Katrina and get her to school. I have a ranch to manage. I'm hoping you'll agree to stay and help me. Temporarily, of course—until I find someone more suitable at the agency."

Poppy shook her head. The guy was not winning any favor points with his explanation. "I see no reason to help you, considering I'm *unsuitable*. Rather ugly word for someone who needed my help."

"I'm sorry. I don't mean your skills or your experience, I meant your age and gender are unsuitable. Or the combination of the two," he said, getting more and more flustered with each attempt to explain.

"Again, another insult. I can safely assure you this conversation is over." Poppy needed a place to stay and figure out where to go from here. She did not have time for Jordan's nonsense.

"I'll pay you double the salary, and all room and board expenses. You can stay in the bunkhouse, and you'll have the whole place to yourself."

The terms were not nonsense, or at least not anything she could not consider. Drat the man. "Why the bunkhouse? That's not exactly a live-in housekeeper. Is it a dumpy place?"

"It's only got the bare-bones necessities, but it's clean and spacious. Having you out there means we aren't crossing any imaginary propriety lines in the eyes of town folks. It also means I don't have to worry about whether you're close enough to help Katrina whenever needed, yet not confusing her. She's at an impressionable age." He leaned back in his chair, his gaze never leaving her.

Poppy had to admire a man who cared about his daughter as much as Jordan seemed to. First in her care, and second in raising her with a moral compass. Double the money was not such an awful offer either. It would give her time to figure out where she was going next and to pocket some extra money without having any expenses of her own. She would be a fool to turn it down.

"Done," she answered quickly, unwilling to give herself time to talk her way out of it. *It was a good offer—even if temporary.*

The lines of tension on Jordan's face slowly eased until they were nonexistent. "Thank you for saying yes, and I'm glad to hear we are on the same page. There's even a spare truck you can drive to take Katrina to school and run errands."

The server delivered their burgers and Poppy took a huge bite. Propriety, schomeity. She did not care about dainty and proper when it came to food—and hunger. She nodded in agreement, loving the idea of a set of wheels and the extra dose of freedom that came with it. In the city, there were buses and taxis, but here in Lincoln, she had not seen a single one of either since her arrival. "How long do you expect me to stick around?" she asked, trying to lay out the details in her head and grateful for the time to make new arrangements.

"It took me two weeks to find you. Although, with the photo mix-up, I'm thinking of changing agencies."

"So you believe me now?" Poppy asked, one eyebrow shooting up in disbelief.

"I do. Your resume is impeccable, although with short teaching stints. The recommendations were solid. And after talking with you, I'm even more comfortable with the new arrangement."

"I'm glad one of us is." She grinned. "For me, getting the job I was hired for would be way more satisfying." The prospect of leaving town in two weeks did not appeal to her, but two weeks was far better than two days.

Jordan went tight-lipped at her obvious dig. "And for me, getting an older woman would be more satisfying. My daughter needs structure and care, not a new mother."

"Point taken." Poppy's earlier opinion of her new employer dropped a notch. A child needed love, and more was better. "Where's Katrina's mother, if you don't mind me asking?"

"I do mind, but it's better for you to know the truth. I'm a widower. Which around here, that word is like catnip to a cat." The man had way too much confidence about his appeal, but unfortunately, or fortunately, depending on how you looked at it, he was probably right.

"It's a good thing I'm a dog person then," she said, delivering the dig in a light teasing tone so as not to push her new boss too far.

"Good." He nodded. "Finish up and I'll take you to the farm where you can meet my daughter. Mrs. Bixby has to leave soon."

They ate the rest of their lunch, small talk on the menu. Jordan did not give away much about himself, but he certainly had a lot of information about Lincoln as he filled her in on the town, trying to help her understand what was expected.

As they drove down the dusty gravel driveway, Poppy was impressed with the main house as it came into view. It was more cabin than a traditional house, but still large, and the front porch welcoming with its rocking chairs and ceiling fans.

Jordan put the car in park. "Welcome to Perry Farms."

"It's a gorgeous place. So quaint and yet...big at the same time. Who designed it?"

"I did." Another surprising piece of information, but there was no time to ask him about it as they got out of the car headed for the porch.

Jordan pushed open the front door and stepped inside, expecting her to follow.

"Daddy, you're home!" A little girl came flying into the room and into Jordan's arms, her blonde pixie braids flopping the whole way.

Jordan scooped her up and hugged her tight. "I sure am, Kitty Kat. Were you good for Mrs. Bixby?" he asked, glancing up at the older woman as she came into the room.

"Oh, Daddy, you know I'm always good," Katrina answered, framing his face with her two hands to plant a kiss on his cheek.

"I do at that." He laughed, the sound pleasing and warm.

The older woman nodded in agreement as she reached for her coat. "I'm sorry, but I really need to get going. I've still got to pack and finish a few errands before I can leave town. It looks like you found someone to help. That makes me feel so much better," the woman declared.

"I did." He nodded. "Alice and Katrina, meet Poppy Delacorte."

"Poppy? Isn't that the woman you went to pick up in the first place?" Alice asked, giving Poppy the once-over and then nodding, as if she'd summed her up in split seconds and found Poppy acceptable. It was more than a little disconcerting.

"It is. We've negotiated our arrangement for the time being," Jordan said, setting his daughter down.

"Poppy's a pretty name, like you." There was nothing awkward or shy about the five-year-old with an award-winning smile.

"Thank you. I love your braids." She kneeled to Katrina's level. "Did you do those?"

"Of course not, silly. I'm too young. Mrs. Bixby did them." She pulled at both braids, holding them up for inspection.

"How lovely to have someone do that for you. They remind me of a hairstyle a princess or a fairy would wear. And Katrina is such a beautiful name. Lucky girl." It was exotic and sounded like something a princess would be named, unlike her own name. Poppy. It was a flower; some even called it a weed.

"Daddy calls me his Kitty Kat, and you can call me Kat if you like. I love cats. There's even one in the barn. Daddy lets me take it food every day, but he won't let me have it in the house. Some no-cat rule I don't like." Katrina pouted as she looked up at her father, placing her hands on her hips for effect.

Poppy could not help but remember Jordan's comments about cats and she sent him a knowing smile, hiding back a smirk. "Cats can be a lot of work," she teased. "And I'd be honored to call you Kat. Thank you."

"It's nice to meet you, Poppy, but I really need to run." The older woman moved toward the door. "Be good for Miss Delacorte, young lady."

"I will. I'm always good." The older woman leaned down to kiss the top of the little girl's head.

"Thanks for helping me out," Jordan said, leaning forward to give the woman a hug. "Enjoy the visit with your daughter and be sure to give her our con-gratulatory wishes when the baby arrives."

"It was nice meeting you, Alice. I'll take good care of Katrina while I'm here, you can be sure of that." Poppy wanted to reassure the woman who clearly cared for both Jordan and the little girl.

"While you're here?" the woman asked, her smile disappearing and turning into a frown.

"Yes. You see, there was a mix-up and Mr. Perry, Jordan, that is, wanted another older woman and instead got me. I'm just here till he finds someone more suitable," she said, unable to resist the teasing barb by drawing reference to his earlier comment.

"Age has nothing to do with ability, Jordan. She seems like a lovely young woman. You might give her a chance to dispel your silly notion before you place another ad."

"I'll think about it," he said, the words giving lie to the firm set of his jaw that declared he'd do no such thing.

"See that you do. I'm off." Alice waved, pulling the door shut behind her and leaving the three of them standing there. There was an awkward silence for a few moments.

"Come on, Poppy. I want to show you my room, and then I can show you where your room is, and Daddy can bring your stuff." Katrina pulled her by the hand, intending to lead her down the hall.

"Not so fast, Kitty Kat. Poppy won't be staying in the house. I'm going to prepare the bunkhouse for her while you show her your room and around the house. I'll be right back."

"But Daddy, why wouldn't she sleep in our house? Don't you want to sleep in the room next to me? Don't you like me, Poppy?" The girl's radiant smile slipped from her face.

"I do. What's not to like? But your dad and I thought it would be best for me to sleep in the bunkhouse. It gives me more of my own space while I'm here." She had teased the poor man enough and letting him off the hook with his daughter seemed like the right thing to do.

Jordan sent her an appreciative smile. The effect was daunting as it warmed her right down to her toes. Poppy had assured her new employer she was not a cat person and had no interest in catnip, of the plant or male variety.

So why the sudden fluttering of her heart?

It was not something she wanted to dwell on. Not to mention it would be a waste of time since she would be long gone in a couple of weeks, maybe sooner. She would do well to remain focus on what needed to happen in the next step of her life.

Chapter Three

♥

I T HAD NOT TAKEN Jordan long to return, but long enough for Katrina to make Poppy feel warm, welcome, and wanted. The little girl bounced from one part of her room to the next, making sure Poppy met all her stuffed animals, commented on all her artwork hanging on the walls, and made sure she was introduced to her mother, albeit through the photo on her bedside table. Katrina's eyes were lit with a mixture of joy and sadness when she had made the final introduction. It was as though she longed to talk about her mother and missed her very much. Poppy knew better than to ask questions, letting Katrina tell her as much or as little as she wanted.

Joining them in the living room, he handed her a key. "That's the key to the bunkhouse. You'll have the place to yourself for the duration of your stay. I've turned on the heat, made up the bed, and put your things in the bedroom. Any questions?"

"Thank you. I'm sure it will be perfect, and no questions at the moment, but if I do, I'll ask." She had not planned on staying in a bunkhouse. For that matter, she was not entirely sure what it meant, but it had to be better than the tiny, cramped apartment she could afford back in Whittling.

"I'm not sure perfect is a good qualifying adjective, but adequate should work." Jordan laughed. It was good to see the tension between them from earlier was gone as it would make the next couple of weeks easier.

"I'll be the judge. Later. Right now, if you could show me around and give a brief overview of the schedule, I might then turn my attention to what to cook for dinner," she offered. It was all very homey and even if temporary, she looked forward to it. It beat sitting alone night after night, only talking to herself. As much as she would have loved to have a pet to keep her company, it was not possible. At least not until she was more settled.

"You don't have to worry about making dinner tonight. You just got here. Kitty Kat and I will figure something out if you think you could survive my cooking." This was something she had not expected from the aloof cowboy.

"Last night, he burnt our pizza. I vote for Poppy to cook," Katrina said, rolling her eyes at her father.

"Thanks for outing me," Jordan said, shooting Poppy a wink. "I thought that was our little secret."

"It was, excepting now we have Poppy. She's got to be a better cook. Right, Poppy?" The little girl looked up at her expectantly. She had never had someone believe in her quite the way Katrina did, and they'd only just met. Two weeks and they would be besties. Something that would make it harder to leave, but something Poppy would enjoy far too much to nix it. *Not even close.*

"I don't know how good a cook I am, but I haven't had any burnt complaints lodged against me." Poppy grinned, joining in the banter.

"See, Daddy. Let her cook. And she can teach me. Right, Poppy?"

"Right, Kat. I'd love to teach you to cook. We'll have to see what we can rustle up for dinner." The image of the two of them cooking side by side, laughing and sneaking bites, was all so Hallmarkish. Poppy's favorite channel.

"Rustle up? Are you sure you're a city girl?" Jordan teased.

"It was my attempt at humor. Can't say as I've used the expression before." If she was going to be here a few weeks, the least she could do was make it fun. For Katrina, herself, and Jordan.

"So, for the tour. Down the hall to the right is a guest bedroom. To the left is my room, but I can take care of it myself."

"I like the sound of that." She laughed. "It means I don't have to do your laundry, so it's one less thing on my to-do list."

"I'm a big boy who knows how to get my laundry to the washroom, unlike another person in this room, no names mentioned." He grinned, shooting a wink in Poppy's direction.

"He means me." Katrina giggled. "Daddy tells me I'm messy and to pick up my stuff all the time. I try, but it's not easy. But with Poppy here, she can help me. Right, Poppy?" The little girl moved to stand next to Poppy, taking her hand to solidify the deal.

"Right, Kat," Poppy said, giving her hand a squeeze. She did not mind; after all, that is what she was hired to do, and for Katrina, she'd be more than happy to help.

"Wrong, Kitty Kat. Poppy's here to look after you, keep up with the house, and cook our meals, *not* clean up behind you. That's your responsibility," Jordan said, his voice firm and fatherly.

Katrina scrunched up her face. "Awww, Daddy. What's the fun of 'sponsibility or whatever that word is?"

"It can be fun if you let it. That's what I'll show you while I'm here," Poppy interjected, trying to keep the peace and to keep her new charge happy.

"I like fun," Katrina said, her smile firmly back in place as they entered the living room.

"The kitchen is back through this door," Jordan said, leading the way.

Far better than she expected, the gleaming white, black, and tan granite counters were uncluttered and large enough to hold a banquet on. Black stainless-steel appliances and an island that included a sink beckoned her to move forward and admire the design. For a guy who did not cook, he'd spared no expense on the kitchen. "This is amazing."

"I'm glad you approve. Kitty Kat's mom loved to cook and even though she never lived here, I designed a kitchen worthy of her approval." Jordan's voice had taken on a tone of sorrow laced with regret.

Poppy could almost feel his pain as it radiated across the room. "That's a sweet sentiment. I'm sure she would have loved it."

"Anyway, feel free to investigate and let me know if there's anything at all that you need." His remark put an end to the discussion about his wife. It was obvious both Katrina and her father had loved Regina Perry with all their hearts, and that the woman had been wanted and cherished. Lucky woman from that aspect.

It was the same thing Poppy dreamed about for herself one day.

"I'm sure you have everything I'll need. Why don't you let me get settled in at the bunkhouse? And then I'll be right back to work on supper. I can tidy up the place a bit while I'm at it." Action would help take her mind off things she had tried to forget—like the most recent dashed hopes of a family centered around her ex. Too bad she hadn't seen through his façade.

"It's your first night. I didn't intend for you to jump right in," Jordan said, repeating the sentiment and making a believer out of Poppy. He had really meant it.

"It's easier this way." Poppy nodded, sending him a gentle smile. "And Kat and I can get to know one another as we work together. Trust me, it's all good."

"If you're sure."

"I'm sure," she said, reaffirming it would be okay and putting his resistance to the idea to rest.

"Yippee. I'm so glad you came to live with us Poppy, even if Daddy is making you stay in the yucky old bunkhouse."

"There's nothing wrong with the bunkhouse. Poppy needs a place away from all your incessant chatter," Jordan teased.

Hands on her hips, Katrina turned to her father. "I have a sweater on and I'm not cold, so I'm not chattering." Katrina glared at him, but it did not last. The two shared a bond that transcended words.

Jordan shook his head and laughed. "Chattering is another word for talking too much."

"I don't talk too much. My last nanny said the same thing, but she was wrong. She was on the phone all the time with her boyfriend. She's the one who talked too much, if you ask me," Katrina said, outing her previous nanny.

"Katrina, that's enough. Let's not disrespect your elders." Jordan used his firm fatherly voice, trying to rein in his daughter's willful chastisement of the poor woman not here to defend herself.

"Anytime you want to talk with me is fine, Kat. I'm used to lots of kids being around in the classroom and it would make me feel right at home," Poppy said, once again aiming for some middle ground between father and daughter.

"See, Daddy. I don't talk too much. Poppy said so." Katrina said, with a look of satisfaction. Her cheeks dimpled.

"We'll see if she still says that by the end of the week," Jordan said with a chuckle.

Poppy did not want to think about the end of this week, any more than she wanted to think about the end of next week which would be even worse. "I'll be right back."

Poppy made her way around the house and spotted the building Jordan had described as the bunkhouse. It was not small by any means, and it looked nice enough from the outside. Maybe to Katrina it was not fancy, but the idea of having the whole place to herself held great appeal.

She unlocked the door and entered. With the fading sun, she flipped on the lights to get a better look. Rough hardwood floors, bare necessity furniture that included a rust-colored sofa that had seen better years but was still serviceable, and a couple of mismatched chairs graced the main area. It was clean, but well used over the years by cowboys who would have cared more about a comfy bed than the living room furnishings. After a long day of work, she would not have cared either.

The place simply needed a few touches to make it look homier. She located her luggage, noting the full-size bed with its dark blue comforter looking warm and cozy. Jordan had not only made the bed but turned back the covers. All that was missing was a chocolate laid out on the pillow. She grinned, unloading her suitcases in search of two of her favorite possessions. A Bible and a framed photograph of her parents.

Poppy paused, gazing down at the picture. Absentee parents most of her life, but still, she held out hope one day they would change and instead of seeking exotic flowers, they would seek a relationship with her.

She took the two items to the living room, placing the photograph in a prominent position on the mantel over the fireplace. The end table next to the sofa was the perfect place for her Bible, right next to the horseshoe and wrought-iron lamp.

It made the place look more lived in, at least a little bit.

Returning to the bedroom, she put away the rest of her things in the drawers and in the bathroom and found homes for a few small knickknacks in the bedroom. Checking out the kitchen, she discovered it was quite adequate, but then she doubted she would be using it much if she was cooking meals in the big house.

That is, if Jordan intended her to eat meals with them. There were a lot of things she did not know yet, and the first order of business was to discuss his expectations. Anything worth doing was worth doing right.

Poppy finished tidying up and then stopped to run a brush through her hair. Satisfied with her appearance, she headed back to the main cabin, locking the door behind her. Out here, she could not imagine she needed to lock it, but ingrained habits were hard to kick.

She knocked at the front door, unsure what to do. It would have been more awkward to simply walk in, at least until she felt comfortable doing so.

Jordan opened the door and stood there, a confused look on his face. "Poppy, what are you doing? Come in. You certainly don't have to knock," he said, as though figuring out the issue.

"Thanks. It just felt weird to walk in." She shrugged, stepping inside and past him, but not before his cologne registered. A woodsy, earthy kind of scent she enjoyed.

"Katrina's in her room. I think she's drawing you a picture. You've made quite an impression on her already. In case I don't get the chance to say this again, I can't thank you enough for helping me out."

"No problem. And I hope you're right about the picture. I love the drawings children give me. I keep a box with every one of them that I've received since I started teaching."

"That must be quite a big box," he said, chuckling.

"Not as many as you think. I've only been teaching for five years and kindergartners love to take pictures home to mommy and daddy. I got more apples than pictures. Must be why I'm so healthy," she teased. All her knickknacks were actually gifts from the children, which was why she adored them.

"Yes, I realize that now, and it should have been a big clue something was up with your application. I reckon I needed you desperately, and so I wasn't hashing out the finer points that didn't add up. But then, you could have been an older woman who discovered late in life a passion for teaching and went back to school." He grinned, trying hard to explain away the error slipping past his guard. Clearly, Jordan liked to think he was in control of everything.

Poppy was stuck on the 'needed you desperately' part, and it took her a few seconds to catch up to his humor. She smiled. "At least you believe me now. Maybe you should pay closer attention to the applications going forward," she said, taking full advantage of the opportunity to one-up him.

"I'll do that." Jordan nodded, a slight grin on his face.

An awkward silence fell between them. "Do you think that while we have a few minutes you can go over your normal routine and let me in on your expectations?" she asked.

"Sure thing. I've written down a list of all the important numbers and addresses. School, doctors, my cell number. That sort of thing." He led her to the dining room and took a seat, gesturing she do the same.

"Thanks, this will be a big help," Poppy said, glancing over the list. She liked the fact he was prepared and had a good handle on what was needed. Katrina was a lucky girl to have such a caring father.

"She has to be to school by eight-thirty and picked up at one-thirty. Kindergarteners have shorter days than the other kids. I send her with a packed lunch and a snack. Usually a sandwich, pre-cut vegetables, that sort of thing. And fruit for a snack. There isn't a fruit she doesn't like that I know of."

Poppy laid the paper down on the table. "It sounds like you stick to a healthy meal plan. I like that and it makes things easy. You can't even begin to imagine some of the snacks parents send their kids to school with."

"Trust me, I've heard all about those snacks. Katrina will try to convince you to join in the other-kids-get-these-snacks game when you go into town shopping." Jordan had a good handle on his daughter and parenthood. The idea he was doing it alone impressed her even more. Her heart went out to him, knowing it could not be easy.

"I'll keep that in mind when I plan your meals as well."

"Dessert never hurt anyone," he said, his smile crinkling the corners of his eyes.

"A man with a sweet tooth. That makes two of us." Kids brought her special food treats and as a result, she had garnered several recipes over the years. She couldn't wait to impress Jordan with her culinary skills. Cooking for herself, she had learned a few tricks along the way, guaranteed to make any meal a success.

"To answer the rest of your questions about expectations, it would be great if the coffee was set for 5:00 a.m., the stronger, the better. I'll be out of the house before you arrive and can take care of my own breakfast. I'm gone most of the day, and home around six. We generally eat around then, and afterward, I try to spend time with Katrina. You're always welcome to join us. Her bedtime is at eight." That answered quite a few of her lingering questions, but it didn't tell Poppy his opinion on the idea of her joining them for meals. It was one thing to offer, another to know which way he preferred.

"Hi, Poppy. Daddy still treats me like a baby. No one in my class goes to bed that early. It would be great if you could tell him to let me stay up later," Katrina said as she entered the room, having overheard her father's remark.

"What time do you think is fair?" Poppy asked, trying to maintain a level of seriousness.

"Oh, hmmm." She tapped her finger against her mouth as if giving the matter thought. "I think midnight. What do you think, Poppy?" she asked, coming to stand next to her.

"Well, I think midnight is far too late, but maybe, if you get up on time and keep your room clean, I might be able to talk your dad into eight-thirty." The art of compromise went a long way toward steering children into making responsible choices. A juggling act for sure, but one she employed with great success with her students.

"You mean it?" Katrina asked.

"I do. But you must do your part first. Deal?" Poppy asked.

"It's a deal." Katrina put out one hand and they shook on it. "And look," she added, holding up a drawing, "I drew you a picture. I didn't know if you ride horses, so I put you on Isabella. She's our oldest horse, but I love her so much. I can share her with you."

"I love this. It's so beautiful and I will treasure it always. Thank you. I don't ride, but maybe one day you can show me how you ride when your daddy is around."

"Okay, I'm real good at it. I'll teach you. What's for dinner?" she asked, switching gears.

"I'm not sure yet. How about you and I go find something and let your daddy relax. He's got a big day at work tomorrow," Poppy said, ignoring the offer to be taught how to ride. It had nothing to do with Katrina being the teacher, and everything to do with her fear of the oversize beasts.

"Daddy doesn't work. He rides horses all day. He's got a fun job," Katrina said in all sincerity, causing Poppy to laugh.

Jordan shook his head. "I'll have you know what I do is hard work, young lady. I don't just ride horses. I fix fences, move cattle, keep up with the property maintenance. Sunup to sundown. The idea of a relaxing evening sounds good to me."

"If you say so." Katrina shrugged. Jordan's attempt to sound indignant was a complete failure.

The art of compromise. "Maybe someday you could show her what you do," Poppy suggested. "Then she could appreciate it more."

Jordan thought about for a few seconds, a sudden light appearing in his eyes. "I could, but that would require you to come with us. Katrina would need supervision."

No way. Her efforts to offer a compromise between the two had backfired. On her. "Oh. Well, in that case, I don't ride, so..."

"Tell her, Daddy. I can teach her, right?"

"She's right, and I'd be right there as well. Consider it your turn to learn something." Jordan had cornered her right and proper.

"Perfect. I can't wait." Poppy was not sure what she was getting into, other than trying to keep Katrina happy. The little girl was beaming, and Poppy realized her exuberance was catchy.

"I'll take you both out on Saturday, but before that, we can give Poppy a couple of basic riding lessons. She might need lots of help, so we can both teach her," Jordan teased.

"That's a good idea, Daddy." Katrina nodded.

"I'm glad you approve. Now run along and help Poppy, but don't get in her way. We don't want her running back to town her first night here." He sent a wink Poppy's way, letting her know he was teasing.

"I wouldn't dream of leaving. After all, I've got the bunkhouse all to myself," she declared.

"Good thing it's not harvesting season, or you'd have about ten other guys sharing it with you."

"But if that was the case, you'd be staying with them and I'd have the house," Poppy joined in the fun, unable to resist. A nightly dose of laughter was something a person could get used to.

Jordan chuckled. "You're probably right. You did say you didn't like cats."

The reminder of their conversation about cats brought her back to reality. This was a job. One that came with preset boundaries and a close friendship with her boss wasn't one of them.

"You don't like cats?" Katrina asked, looking up at her in confusion.

"I do. Your daddy doesn't know what he's talking about." Let him mull over that comment while she worked on dinner. It would be just enough to keep him slightly off-kilter.

He was talking about women, while she, on the other hand, was referring to the feline variety. In fact, she loved all animals, and one day, she had promised herself a pet. Thinking of her life in two suitcases and two bags, she did not have much of anything to call her own, and now simply wasn't the right time.

Chapter Four

♥

THE NEXT FEW DAYS, they fell into a routine—Katrina and Poppy growing closer with each passing hour. True to his word, Jordan was gone most days, but at night they shared dinner together, typically followed by a game, and sometimes a movie. It was all very familyish and fun. And much to her consternation, Poppy found herself watching for Jordan to come home, enjoying the conversations with him as much as those with Katrina. The first night had been a huge success, paving the way to a happy coexistence.

Poppy had put together a spaghetti dinner worthy of a chef. It was not ordinary sauce from a jar and noodles slopped together. Instead, she had started with the jar of sauce due to time limitations and added fresh ingredients. Tomatoes, zucchini, squash, mushrooms, and onions followed by lots of spices. The result was a masterpiece of mouth-watering sauce atop perfectly cooked noodles and a side garden salad to complement it. Katrina and Jordan had thoroughly enjoyed the meal and verbally shared their enthusiasm, which in turn, made Poppy feel overjoyed at the success. The circle of life at Perry's Farm at been set, and within days, Poppy could not help but wish she didn't have to leave.

Sometimes, life was not fair.

Two weeks was not long, especially if Jordan found someone sooner versus later. It was a bit pretentious on his part to assume every woman would fall in love with him, and therefore, she was determined to prove to him she was different. Not only could she do the job, but she would not fall in love.

And with each day, she learned more about Lincoln, meeting people in the small town, their warm welcome taken with a healthy dose of caution. Poppy knew better than to let them get close for two reasons. One, she was leaving, and it was pointless. Two, because people tended to say one thing and really think and do another. Hypocrisy at its best.

By the fourth day, Poppy considered talking to Jordan. Or rather, bulldoze him in the hopes of convincing him to let her stay. Long afternoon walks had turned into meet-and-greets with the horses, but so far, there had not been time for riding lessons.

Poppy loved Matilda, the stray cat. Whether a house cat or not, the cat loved Katrina, following her around, other than when she was eating of course. The cat lapped up every drop of food the little girl delivered daily.

The farm was quiet, and Poppy was quickly becoming enamored of it all. A multitude of birds flitted from tree to tree in search of food, calling out their sing song chatter. It was astonishing how many Katrina could identify, and how few Poppy knew. They had turned the walks into a game of show and tell—Poppy generally the loser. She had missed a lot of what life had to offer while living in the city, although Katrina was missing out on some of the joys and excitement of city life. There always seemed to be a tradeoff.

After getting Katrina off to school this morning, Poppy started to work on what to serve for dinner. She would have to make another grocery store run when she went back into town if she intended to serve her cream sherry sauce over chicken, another one of her personal favorites. Jotting down a list, she added a few other things to it. It was hard to believe she was nearing the end of her first week, the thought not bringing her much joy.

The back door opened, and Jordan walked in, surprising her. He rarely came home during the day.

"Hey, there. Forget something?" she asked.

"No. I need to talk to you about something," Jordan said, lines of tension creasing his forehead.

She had tried so hard to make things perfect for him and his daughter and she couldn't imagine where she'd messed up. "You sound serious. Did I do something wrong?"

"No. Not at all. You've done an amazing job, and Katrina is already half in love with you." Jordan smiled, leaning back against the kitchen counter, arms crossed in front of his chest. "Can I ask you something?"

"Sure. My life is an open book," she said, fully expecting more digging into her past and her qualifications.

Jordan nodded, seemingly pleased with her answer. "Why all the moving around and changing jobs?"

Just as she expected, although disappointing "It's a fair question, but I'm not sure how it pertains to what I'm doing now if you're satisfied with my efforts."

"True." He nodded. "It's just that something has come up and it looks like I need to change our original deal. I know you mentioned looking for work elsewhere and was wondering where you stand on the issue." His gaze remained intent on her.

Jordan wanted her to leave. Plain and simple. The only explanation she could think of was that he resented the bond forming between her and Katrina. It was a heartbreaking thought considering she felt the opposite.

"I was alone a lot as a child because my parents traveled extensively and were always out of the country. I tried not to get connected to people and places, knowing stability wasn't something I could count on. As an adult, I began to apply the same principle. Whenever I discover that the people around me are not what I expect, I leave, hoping to one day find a place to call home. A place where people are real. And no, I haven't found a job yet, although there is a teaching job in New York I'm waiting to hear back on. What exactly did you mean about reworking our arrangement?" She might as well know when he wanted her gone. She had let her guard down and let herself start to care more than she should of—for Katrina and Jordan.

"I got a job offer this morning. One I find hard to turn down. Mack Mitchell, one of our local cattle ranchers needs to move his cattle and one of his ranch hands broke a leg yesterday. He's asked me to ride with him, and the money is considerable. The farm has been struggling this year, what with the drought wreaking havoc on the crops."

"How does that concern me?" she asked, unsure where he was going with this discussion.

"I was hoping you'd agree to stay a little longer. I'd need you to move into the cabin to stay with Katrina. I'd be gone close to a week and half as they move two herds to new pastures. They're real cattle drives, but as a dude ranch there are some novices that slow the process down and they need experienced outriders to keep it all under control."

He did not want her to leave. She breathed a sigh of relief, her mind spinning with joy. "I've always thought it would be fun to vacation at a dude ranch. How exciting. And to think they're going pay you instead of vice versa. But why would I need to stay longer than a few days extra, not that I'm complaining. Just wondering."

"Because on the cattle drive, I won't have time to find someone to replace you. If you could stay an extra week or two that would be great. I didn't have any luck finding anyone yet."

Her joy slipped down a notch or two. It was only a temporary reprieve. "Seeing as I have nowhere to go, I'd love to stay." It would give her more time to change Jordan's mind, and if that failed, time to find a new job, perhaps even in Lincoln. The quaint town was growing on her, although she still was not sure small-town living was her style. The conveniences offered in the city with everything at her fingertips was a much better option for someone in her situation. As in—no car.

He nodded. "You're a lifesaver. I can't begin to thank you enough, given the circumstances. "I'll leave you the keys to the truck, and our next-door neighbor, Harriet Collins, will look in on you every day."

This just kept getting worse. Not only was it still temporary, but it was also monitored supervision. She was beginning to regret her haste in agreeing. "As in you don't trust me. I get it."

Jordan frowned. "It's not that at all. You came with glowing references, and I've watched you with Katrina this past week. Harriett will stop by to see if you need anything. My words meant exactly what I said. Don't try and read anything into my motives."

"Well, okay, then," Poppy said, his words putting her in her place.

"I've got to get back to work. I leave at the crack of dawn and there's much to be done to prepare for my absence. And if you don't mind, I'd like to be the one to tell my daughter. She has separation issues ever since her mother passed away, and she won't like this one bit. I hate that I need to leave her, but the money will come in handy."

"I won't say a word. She and I will be just fine, trust me." Jordan nodded and strode out of the kitchen without so much as a backward glance.

Poppy did a fist pump. It was not long-term, but it was more time to prove to Jordan she could both do the job and not fall in love with him. Maybe then he would ask her stay.

Permanently.

Chapter Five

❤

POPPY WANDERED DOWN THE hall in search of coffee, the fresh aroma guiding her to the kitchen. This morning, there was plenty left for since Jordan had left at dawn. He had said his goodbyes to Katrina the night before, his daughter hugging him tightly before announcing that she and Poppy would have everything under control and not to worry. It had been amusing to listen to a five-year-old trying to sound all grown up.

After Katrina had gone to bed, Jordan had gone over detailed instructions of what each day should look like, and it was no surprise that next to the coffee pot there was a complete list of everything he had already told her. The man was a worrywart, but his daughter was lucky to have someone who loved her whole-heartedly.

Poppy poured a cup of coffee and made her way to the table, mulling over his notes as she sat there. Monday through Friday was easy enough. Breakfast. Pack a lunch. Take Katrina to school. Pick Katrina up from school. Homework. The few days she had been in school on Poppy's watch, homework had entailed more coloring and fun. It was the same in the classes she had taught, her perspective one that the introduction to school should always be made fun to ease children into the new world of learning.

Next came dinner. Games or G-rated movie. Bedtime sharply at eight. Saturday was filled with suggestions on how to entertain his daughter, as though Poppy could not come up with any ideas of her own. She had had a nanny and knew plenty of what could be done based on her own experience. It was more a case of what not to do, as Poppy's nanny left a lot to be desired. While her botanist parents were always off chasing some exotic flower in foreign lands, she had been left with the thorn bush in the form of a nanny.

Day after day, as a child she had imagined what it would be like to have a nanny be kind to her. Poppy knew all the things she wanted to with Katrina, things she had wanted someone to do with her, but never got. Jordan had written down coloring, games, outdoor walks, and a picnic. The first two the child did all week. Being outside would hold a lot more interest for Katrina and Poppy, but it would include way more fun than a simple walk and picnic.

Poppy smiled to herself, picked up the pen, and added a few notes to the Saturday options. Sunday was church, and although she preferred not to attend, she would go for Katrina's sake. Her experience with church people never seemed to leave her with the warm fuzzies. It was a case of 'do what I say, not what I do.' In Whittling, she thought things were finally going to be different; until she realized that was only until you said no to the town's golden boy quarterback who just so happened to be the deacon's son. Of course, no matter what she said to the contrary, they believed him.

Rupert Jones was the fine upstanding young man who had grown up in Whittling, not some stranger who moved to town a short year ago. But he was not the first one to turn her against the church. Her nanny had done a fair job of that early on. Millicent Beanie and her cronies, always bickering and sneering about someone or another, as though they were perfect. Poppy preferred to secretly think of her as Millicent Meanie.

Poppy's sole comfort had been in reading God's word and praying to herself each night. God had seen her through the dark days, and she trusted He would always be there for her when she needed Him most.

Like now.

She did not want to move again. At thirty, she wanted to settle down. But once again, it did not seem like it was going to happen.

Poppy looked up as Katrina came into the kitchen, rubbing her eyes.

"Good morning, Kat. You're up earlier than normal."

"Good morning. Is my daddy gone yet? I wanted to say bye," she said, a big yawn taking over her sentence.

"He has, I'm afraid. But last night you gave him extra special goodbyes and I'm sure you'll get to talk to him when he's not busy." Katrina was looking slightly pensive about his leaving now that it had occurred. A far cry from last night's assurances.

"Okay. What's for breakfast?" She sat next to Poppy, nudging her chair closer.

"I thought I'd make you some special Mickey Mouse pancakes. I used to dream of getting them on special occasions."

"Did you? Get them, I mean. I love pancakes, but I haven't had the Mickey Mouse kind," Katrina said, her eyes wide as saucers.

"I didn't but dreaming about something is good too. My nanny didn't know how to make them." Or more than likely, went out of her way not to make them. That would have been too much work for crotchety woman.

"You had a nanny? Just like me. That's cool. I don't think dreaming about pancakes will taste near as good as the real thing in my tummy." There had been nothing cool about her nanny, but it wasn't anything Katrina needed to know.

"I reckon you're right. Do you want to help me make them so you can learn too?"

"Can I?" Katrina asked; the wonder in her voice a dead giveaway she did not get to help out in the kitchen much. But then, it did not sound like Jordan was much of an expert in the kitchen himself, so teaching a child would be disastrous.

"Absolutely." For Poppy, this would be the fun she did not have as a child. The pancakes were thirty years in the making, but they would the best pancakes ever because they were shared with a child whose joy was overflowing.

"What's that?" Katrina asked, pointing at the paper Poppy held.

"It's a list of your daddy's instructions for us while he's gone. I've added a few things of my own to our fun list."

"What kinds of things? I can't read yet."

"Fun things like an outdoor adventure, a magical tent, a tea party, crafting, and I thought we could some make some cookies and decorate them." She pointed at each item she had added to give the child a sense of what the words looked like.

"Wow. This is going to be the best week ever. Maybe you should come live with us forever. I don't want another nanny, I want you." She nodded. "And I'm going to tell my daddy when he gets home."

Poppy laughed. "We'll see if you still think that by the time your dad comes back. But I assure you, whoever your dad finds will be perfect. He loves you very much and would only hire the best."

"He hired you and you're the best. So why do you need to leave?" Katrina had lots of questions and ideas Poppy was not qualified to answer.

"It's hard to explain, but your dad has it in his head who he wants for you long term."

"Then he needs to change his head." Katrina frowned.

"Let's go make pancakes, we don't want you to be late for school." Poppy ruffled the girl's hair playfully.

Smile back in place, Katrina moved to the panty and pulled out a stool to stand on. Poppy gathered all the ingredients and measured them into the bowl, letting Katrina do the mixing.

"Sorry," Katrina said, looking up at Poppy, a worried frown on her face.

Flour had landed everywhere on the counter, but it would be easily cleaned when all was said and done. "Don't worry about it. Sometimes, making a mess is half the fun."

The little girl shook her head. "That's not what Daddy says. He likes everything clean, including my room." She scrunched up her face in distaste.

"That reminds me, we need to put pick-up game on our list of things to do."

"Okay, I like games. What do we do now?"

"Let me give it a few more quick stirs and then were ready to cook them." It was more like a lot of stirs to get the ingredients all mixed and the flour absorbed into the liquid, but Katrina did not need a lesson in precision. This was about fun.

Poppy heated the griddle, letting Katrina pour out a couple of small circles for the face, while Poppy added the smaller circles for ears.

"This looks awesome. Now what do we do?"

"We wait." Poppy chuckled, knowing the wait was always the hardest part. "Let's set the table. Maybe you could get the silverware—a fork and a butter knife will do."

"I'm not allowed to have a knife. Daddy says I'm not ready. But I'm not a baby."

"I tell you what, you can have a butter knife and I'll watch you carefully. If you do a good job, we can show your daddy you're a big girl. Sharp knives are out of the question, but this is the next step. And only when you're sitting at the table. Deal?"

"Deal," Katrina said, nodding her head and skipping to the silverware drawer and then walking back to the table very slowly, holding the knives and forks out in front of her like they were glass.

Poppy grabbed the whipped cream and the chocolate chips, as well as the maple syrup. Pure syrup and straight from Canada...nothing but the best. "Time to flip," she announced.

Katrina came rushing over and stepped on the stool. "Can I do it?"

"How about I show you how to do this on the first one and then you decide. We have to be super careful not to burn ourselves or to break the ears off."

Katrina frowned. "Maybe you should do both. I don't like to get burned. I did once before on a pan, and it hurt for days."

"Okay, but eventually, you'll be ready, and you just need to say the word," Poppy said, trying to encourage the little girl. It was okay to be afraid, if she did not let her control her and shy away permanently. When the time was right, she would overcome her fears. Poppy could not help but wish she'd be there to see it.

With the pancakes finished, Poppy opened the bag of chocolate chip, placing several in a circle to make the eyes.

"That's so cool." Katrina beamed.

"Watch this." Poppy took the whipped cream and sprayed a curved line for the mouth and then dropped a few more chocolate chips in a straight line.

Katrina giggled, the sound sweet music. "It looks like he's got rotten teeth."

"You're right. I think he forgot to brush." Poppy grinned down at Katrina, the two of them heading to the table where she set the plates down. "Time to eat. Do you want a little syrup drizzled on him?"

"Yummy. Yes, please." Katrina's voice was soft and sweet, touching a chord within Poppy.

"Hmmm. These are good."

"I have to agree." Poppy chuckled. It was a treat she would make again—soon.

When they finished eating, Poppy took the plates to the sink. "Better hurry up and get dressed and ready for school. It won't do to be late."

"Will you pick out my clothes? That would be fun."

"Sure thing, give me a minute to rinse these and I'll be right there." Katrina had a way of making her feel wanted and it was a feeling Poppy was quickly getting used to. As a teacher, some of the children made her feel special. But this was the undivided attention of a little girl who acted as though she hung the moon. For days—not hours.

Picking out clothes had been easy, Katrina's wardrobe overflowing with beautiful outfits. Something else Poppy did not have an abundance of in her childhood. Uniforms for school. And the rest—just house clothes and, of course, church clothes.

After dropping off Katrina at school, Poppy stopped at the store for more groceries and then headed back to the cabin, determined to make sure it was spotlessly clean. And she busied herself in search of what they would need for the big event she planned for tonight's entertainment, hoping Katrina would love it as much as she herself would. Being a nanny to Katrina was giving her the chance to live her childhood the way she had been denied, and the evening's entertainment was another one on the never-ever-have-I-done list. It was magical tent night.

The day passed quickly and soon she was back in the pickup line at school, waiting for Katrina. The woman came to the car, looked down at her clipboard, and smiled.

"Ms. Delacorte, right?" the woman asked, sizing her up.

"Yes. I'm here for Katrina Perry."

"Yes, yes, my dear. Let me call for her. Katrina Perry, please. Line 1," the woman said into her walkie talkie. "I heard Jordan left on a cattle drive and that you're taking care of his daughter by yourself. Bless your heart, it was a good thing he had you there. He's a hard worker, that man is. Easy on the eyes, too, if you know what I mean." The woman grinned.

"I hadn't noticed. The easy-on-the-eyes part," she corrected. "He's definitely a hard worker." The last thing she wanted to do was discuss Jordan on a personal level with a stranger. Or anyone at all, for that matter.

"Been a rough year on the farmers with the drought and all. That man needed to catch a break. He also needs to catch a woman if you know what I mean." The woman eyed Poppy with sudden interest.

Poppy shook her head. "Don't go getting any ideas. I think he's quite content with his current status quo, as am I."

Katrina came skipping up to the truck alongside a teacher who opened the back door and helped her climb in. "Hi, Poppy. Today was so much fun." The little girl's eyes were filled with excitement.

"Have a nice day, you two. Think about what I said," the older woman grinned, stepping back. The teachers waved as Poppy pulled away, making sure the line kept moving. It was also a great way to end the conversation.

"I'm glad you had a good day. What did you do?"

"We played Dodge ball and my team won. Isn't that cool?" Katrina said, a broad smile on her face.

"It sure is. But more important than winning was the team spirit and fun you had, right?"

"Yes, I guess." She shrugged. Winning was not everything but Poppy would save the lecture for Jordan to have with her. Poppy only wanted fun for the next week.

"What did Mrs. Burke want to talk about? Did I do something wrong? What did she want you to think about?" Katrina asked.

Poppy shook her head as she glanced in the rearview mirror. "You haven't done anything wrong, sweetheart. She wanted me to think about what kind of fun we could have tonight."

"And what's that?" she asked, her eyes and face all aglow.

"It's magical tent night." Poppy shot Katrina a grin and was rewarded with a huge smile.

"Yay. I've always wanted to build a magical tent. This will be the best night ever."

Poppy caught the enthusiasm, letting it fill her to overflowing and her own personal level of anticipation for the evening. "Well, then, tonight's your magical night where dreams come true."

"Yay!" Katrina exclaimed.

They drove the short way to the house, and Poppy was surprised to notice they had a visitor.

"That's Mrs. Collins from next door. Daddy says she's nosey but nice." Out of the mouths of babes. She would do well to remember anything she said might very well be repeated somewhere down the line.

Poppy laughed. "I don't recommend you say that to anyone else. And I can't believe your daddy would say that to you."

"Oh, he didn't. I overheard him talking to someone on the phone. I think it was because she was trying to get him to date some lady he didn't like. Daddy hasn't dated since...well, you know, since my mom." Katrina's voice had dropped a few notches, the subject of her mother still painful.

"I don't think you should worry a thing about any of it. That's grown-up stuff and I think the only thing you should worry about is having fun." It was obvious their neighbor was one of the matchmaking mama's Jordan had told her about.

"Well, hello. I'm Harriet Collins, Jordan's neighbor. He asked me to stop in and check on you daily while he's away. Is everything going, okay?" She glanced at Katrina who bounded up the front steps.

"Hi, I'm Poppy Delacorte. It's nice to meet you. And yes, everything is going great. Katrina makes that easy. She's such a sweet child."

Harriet looked her up and down, her open assessment reminding her far too much of the looks she had received right before leaving Whittling. Looks that said they had her all figured out and found her wanting. "Yes, if you say so. My daughter adores her, and she and Jordan are quite close. It's a shame she couldn't drop everything and come help him out. I don't know why he insists on bringing in other women."

Poppy knew exactly what she meant by other women. *Competition.* "I don't know either." It was easier not to get drawn into Jordan's personal affairs. She glanced up at the sky, noticing the dark, luminous clouds rolling in. "Looks like we're in for a heck of a storm."

"Yes, yes. I heard we could get up to an inch and a half. Will be good for the farm if it doesn't do any damage. I reckon I should get home before it starts raining buckets."

"Thanks for stopping by," Poppy said, smiling. She would not let the woman's attitude rob her of the fun she intended to have with Katrina.

School was out and the weekend was here—with fun and more fun on the menu.

Chapter Six

♥

"**G**UESS WE CAN'T GO on an adventure walk in the rain. I hate rain 'cause I'm always stuck inside," Katrina said, staring out the front window, one hand on the glass. The clouds had opened up and were dumping buckets of rain.

Poppy made a mental note: clean windowpane. This was no time for moping faces. "Says who?"

"Grownups." Katrina pouted. "I wanted to go see my cat and take her some food and then go on an adventure walk. Who's going to feed her now? Everything is ruined."

Not all grownups and certainly not this one. "Not necessarily. I don't agree with those grownups. As to the cat, I needed some supplies from the barn and I've already taken food out to her. She's such a cutie with her ears and paws looking like she dipped them in black paint. She was super shy, but I figure she'll come around when she gets used to me."

"Thank you. You're the best. But what did you mean about not agreeing with grownups? Don't all grownups say the same thing?" she asked, curious eyes focused on Poppy.

"Nope. To me, if it's at least seventy-five degrees outside, I say it's time to make merry and dance. Rain is a gift from God and should be something to rejoice." She had only done it once, having slipped past her nanny. There had been heck to pay afterward, but Poppy remembered it as well worth it.

"What do you mean?" Katrina moved to stand beside her.

Poppy took her small hands in her own and moved in circles, arms high up. "Dancing in the rain is magical. Come on, I'll show you."

"You mean it?" Katrina asked, as if afraid to believe.

Poppy laughed and twirled Katrina around in a circle. "Of course. It's seventy-six degrees outside. You go swimming, don't you?"

"Well, yeah."

"Pools can be cold, and usually not more than seventy-two degrees unless heated. So, this is no different, only more fun. It's hard to dance in a pool of water." It was the same sound logic she had tried to use with her own nanny, but it didn't wash. The woman did not have an adventurous or fun bone in her body.

"This sounds like fun. Let me get my raincoat."

"None required. You don't wear a raincoat to swim," Poppy said, laughing. "Half the fun is getting soaked, the rain dripping down your face, your hair plastered in chunks."

"Let's go. I want to dance in the rain." Katrina raced for the door.

"Say no more." Poppy took her by the hand and led her outside. This would be a day to remember.

"Now what?" Katrina asked.

"We dance. Dance for Jesus. Make merry." Poppy raised her arms in the air and tilted her face to the sky. Sticking out her tongue to catch the magical drops, she laughed and twirled around.

Katrina soon followed her lead and joined in the merriment. The two of them were thoroughly wet in minutes as the rains poured out from heaven. "Follow me."

Poppy raced down the driveway, stopping only to jump in each puddle, soaking her shoes and pants in the process. The sound of Katrina's laughter brought joy to her heart. This was a perfect moment in time, and one Poppy wished did not have to end.

But as Katrina slowed down, exhausted from their merriment and games, Poppy led her back inside. "Wait here. I'll go fetch us some towels, so we don't track through the house."

"Hurry, I'm cold now." Katrina stayed in the foyer, and Poppy rushed back with the towels.

"Here, wrap one around your hair and make a turban." She grinned as Katrina tried and failed. Pulling a towel around the little girl's shoulders, she then helped her wrap her hair up. "Now we need to shuck our clothes and put on something dry."

"That was so much fun. I probably shouldn't tell Daddy. I don't want him mad at you."

"Never lie, sweetheart. I can handle your father, and there was no harm in what we did. Just always make sure it's warm enough outside so you don't catch cold." It was an old myth and Poppy knew it. It was the same spiel her nanny had given her, but she did not get sick. She was living proof of the lie perpetuated over generations.

"Okay, then. I can't wait to tell him. I don't ever want you to leave, Poppy. I'm going to tell my daddy he needs to keep you." Katrina nodded; as if saying the words would make it happen.

If only it were that easy. But life was not easy, or at least, it hadn't been for Poppy. Maybe if she had had normal parents or even one normal parent, things would have been better. But her parents had preferred exotic flowers and traveling the world over spending time with Poppy. She had overheard them once discussing the situation. It was then she had learned she was not a planned pregnancy. And to a seven-year-old, that equated with unwanted.

"What's next?" Katrina asked.

"I think we should build our magical tent and then take some hot soup and sandwiches in it and have dinner." Poppy shoved aside the unwanted memories, preferring to stay in the current moment filled with laughter and fun. The joy of being a kid.

"Yippee. My own magical tent. Can we sleep in it like people sleep in tents outside? I'm not brave enough to sleep outside, but inside would be so much fun."

"I don't see why not. We just need lots of cozy blankets and pillows. Do you know where your father keeps his Christmas decorations?"

"Christmas?" Katrina asked, pulling on her dry clothes. "Why would we want Christmas decorations? It's summer." Katrina frowned, trying to understand.

Poppy stopped rubbing her hair long enough to answer. "For the lights, silly. A magical tent wouldn't be magical without fairy lights."

"Ohhh. That sounds pretty. Come on, I'll show you where he keeps them."

Poppy rewrapped her hair in the towel and let Katrina lead her down the hall, stopping midway.

"It's all up there. In the attic." She pointed to the ceiling where a trapdoor was framed out. "There's a ladder when you pull it down."

"Perfect. Should be easy enough. You wait right here, and I'll go up to see what I can find."

"Okay. Be careful, Poppy. That's a steep ladder. Daddy won't let me climb it. He says it's too dangerous, but I wouldn't go up anyway. I think it's scary. That's where ghosts would live."

"Your father is right about it being dangerous for you, but I can assure you, there are no ghosts. You wait right here, and I'll go check it out and report back to you." Poppy started to climb the ladder, her thoughts on Jordan.

He was protective, and most of the time Poppy saw it as a positive. Just some things needed slight adjusting in order to make way for fun and learning. A chance to grow without fear. By the time Poppy was sixteen, she had read the Bible over completely seven times. Her parents had brought it back from Italy and she treasured it. Life's lessons were all in there. How to act, how to treat others, everything. It all came down to love, respect, and faith. And in faith, she grew up without fear.

It was the love and respect parts she was having issues with. She wanted to love people and respect them, but it was difficult at best when every time she turned around, people failed her.

"Everything looks a-okay up here. No ghosts in sight."

"Yay. Just hurry and find the lights," Katrina said, only a hint of her earlier fear still vibrating in her voice.

Poppy searched for the boxes labeled Christmas, opening each one to peer inside. The lights turned up in the fifth container, but Poppy couldn't resist looking in the other six. Eleven boxes total just for Christmas. Beautiful painted musical rocking horses, a nativity scene with handcrafted people and a manger, ornaments that included what would seem to be everything Katrina would have made. The list went on, and each item was lovingly stored with care.

Poppy would give anything to see the house all lit up in Christmas splendor.

"I've got them," she said, finally coming down the ladder. "Let's go create our magical home for the night."

Katrina glowed with happiness. "You're the best, Poppy." They moved down the hall toward her bedroom, hand in hand, just like best friends. Something Poppy never had; her nanny not allowing people to visit had quickly shut down the friend chain. Who wanted to be BFFs with a girl who could not play with them half the time?

They entered her bedroom and Poppy led Katrina to the stack of blankets and sheets she had put there early today, along with lots of rope and a couple of poles she'd found in the barn. Poppy eyeballed the room, laying out her strategic points for tie-off points. She took the poles and held one out to Katrina.

"Here. If you hold this up, we can drape a sheet over it and put the other end over your desk chair. We'll tie it off as our main frame and then build off it."

"Right here?" Katrina asked.

"That's perfect." Poppy draped the blanket and tied off two of the corners, and then draped another sheet partly over the first, securing it with clothespins, and two more poles to give it added height. "Okay, nice and easy, come and stand here and hold this one."

"This is really cool. Where did you learn to make a magical tent?"

"It was something I saw on TV once and then I tried it, much to the consternation of my nanny."

"What's constanation?"

"Consternation. It means she didn't like it." Poppy grinned, proof just how much the Katrina effect was having on her. To laugh at the past was a feat unto itself.

"If she didn't like magical tents, she must not have been very nice." Katrina frowned.

"She wasn't." It was the simple truth, but it was as far as she would explain to Katrina. Some things were not meant for a child to hear. Just like when she had heard she was not wanted. Poppy shoved the thought aside, not wanting to think about it now. The ugly thought always reared its head when she found herself at the end of the shoved-aside stick. It was what the church had done because of her ex, and now Jordan was doing it because she was too young. Would she ever be anyone's perfect?

"I'm glad you're nice." Katrina beamed a heart-warming smile in her direction.

"Me too, because so are you."

An hour later, they had everything in place. It was a tent fit for a fairy princess with twinkling lights, fluffy bedding, and large enough for them to sleep and eat. "Almost done."

"Almost? What else is there? I think it's amazing." Katrina's eyes shone with delight as she lay on her bedding and gazed up at the lights.

"Stars. After we eat, of course." Poppy glanced at her watch. "My goodness, it's already seven."

"How do we make stars?"

"We draw them, color them, and then cut them out to hang from the roof of the tent."

"I can't wait."

"Dinner first."

"That's a deal. I'm hungry."

"Me too." They both giggled. Crawling out of the tent, they headed for the kitchen, hand in hand.

Tomato soup and grilled cheese sandwiches rocked the tent setting, as did the seventeen stars they hung up. Seventeen was Katrina's number since that was the day of her birthday. They lay back on the bedding, hand in hand, gazing up at their creation. It was after eleven, way past the little girl's bedtime, but it had been a night to remember.

Chapter Seven

♥

After a late sleep-in on Saturday, Poppy had agreed to leave up the tent. Katrina wanted to show her dad and share the experience with him. The rain had finally quit sometime in the wee hours of the morning, and by afternoon everything was dry enough for an adventure walk. By that time, there was no holding back a rambunctious five-year-old determined to have the best weekend ever.

Their walk took them down by the creek, the water rushing after a couple of inches of rain flooded it. When they had returned home, it was to discover Harriet had come by to check on them and became worried when she discovered they weren't at home.

Poppy called her straight away to let her know they were fine and there was no call for alarm. They had spent the rest of the day having fun in the tent, watching movies, and managing a pizza for dinner and a healthy dose of freshly baked cookies as dessert. Never-ending fun.

Today was another story entirely.

It was Sunday. *Church day and Jordan's* orders were for Katrina to attend. It seemed silly to drop the child off and leave. What message would that send? Poppy knew she had to do the right thing and stay for the service. It was only an hour, after all; how bad could it be in a new town where no one knew her?

"Wake up, sleepyhead." Poppy kneeled, brushing back Katrina's hair from her face and dropping a kiss on her forehead. "We need to eat breakfast and get ready for church," Poppy said, tickling Katrina awake and making her laugh.

"But what about our fun? I'd rather stay here with you." *That made two of them.*

Poppy shook her head and smiled. "There'll be plenty of time for that afterward."

"Okay. I can't wait to tell my friends about all the cool things I've been doing." Katrina sat up, pushing back the blankets. "You should have stayed in here again last night. I even hung a moon." Sure enough, she had made a moon and taped it to one of the stars.

Which meant she had done it after Poppy had tucked her into bed. She ought to say something, like to tell her bedtime was for bed, but she did not have the heart.

Katrina's happy smiles made her feel warm and wanted and she had no intention of changing that. "Maybe I will tonight." That way they would both catch up on some sleep.

"Ka chew!" Katrina sneezed, covering her mouth.

"God bless you," Poppy said, handing Katrina a pretty dress to wear to church.

"Do I have to wear a dress? It's not fair, cause then I can't play like the boys," Katrina whined, a pout on her face.

"True enough. Why don't you wear the dress and put shorts under it? It'll be the best of both worlds." Poppy was a master at compromise and leading children down the path they should go, letting it seem like it was their decision.

"Okay, I like it." Katrina smiled at her warmly, her cheery morning attitude firmly back in place.

"Meet you in the kitchen," Poppy said as she left the room.

It was not long before Katrina joined her, looking pretty in pink. Even her shoes were a shiny pink. The overall effect was very princess and regal-like. "Ready."

"You certainly are. Eat your breakfast and I'll have just enough time to brush out your hair before we need to leave.

Katrina sat at the table, hungrily devouring her cereal and toast. After she finished, Poppy rinsed out the dishes and fixed Katrina's hair before they loaded into the truck and drove into town.

Poppy parked in the closest spot she could find, and then escorted Katrina off to children's church and checked her in. The temptation to leave hit her again, but the lure of sweet music coming from the sanctuary had her traveling in a different direction. Poppy sat down toward in one of the back rows in case she wanted a quick exit.

"Good morning, dear. I saw you come in with Katrina. Are you her new nanny?" A kindly, older woman had joined her.

"I am. Poppy Delacorte," she answered, reaching out her hand for the obligatory handshake. There was no reason to mention it was short-term. And it was not as if the woman would be overly interested anyway. She was simply making small talk.

The woman shook her hand. "Jordan certainly found himself a pretty lady to take care of his house and his daughter. Where are you from? Oh, and I'm Susan Beckett."

"Nowhere in particular, although I grew up in up-state New York. I like to travel so I move around a bit. Last stop was Whittling, NY." It was mostly the truth. It was not that she liked to travel, it was that people made her want to leave. On to the next place, each time with high hopes.

"Well, maybe, Lincoln will be a place you could call home. There's so much to do. You could join a small group here at the church. Great way to get to know people. And then there's always the Cattle Corral. That's kind of a hot spot in town for some really good steaks and there's always music and dancing."

"Thanks, I might have to check on it." Code for *not in this lifetime*. The church part, that is. The last thing she wanted was to get involved with people who would never make her feel like a part of the community. She was destined to be an outsider.

"You do that. It's been so nice chatting with you. If you need anything, just let me know. Got to do all I can to make sure you young folk come to town and stick around. 'Specially the nice ones, like yourself. I can tell you've got a good heart." The woman patted her arm, the action disconcerting. It was friendly and hard to resist.

"Thank you. What a sweet thing to say," she managed before the woman walked away, joining an older man that Poppy could only assume was her husband. Caught off guard with the woman's effusive praise, she responded to the overt kindness.

The music was peaceful and the pastor's message full of hope. It was as though he were speaking to her. Poppy wanted to believe hope and love were there for the taking for all believers, but so far, she had not run into it. Or not enough to carry her through the rough times. Only God had been able to do that for her, but it would be nice to experience what she witnessed in others who had family and friends.

At the end of the service, Poppy made her way to the children's area, her progress slow as she was repeatedly stopped by people wanting to say hi, introduce themselves, and welcome her to Lincoln. Bright smiles for a beautiful Sunday. But what happened the rest of the days of the week? Poppy's experience had taught her this was a Sunday façade.

She pushed away the cynicism and pasted on a smile. One that turned into anything but fake when she spotted Katrina, the girl racing toward her. Wrapping her arms around Poppy's waist, Katrina hugged her tight.

"Can we go home now? I'm ready to have more fun. With you. Promise me you'll never leave, Poppy."

"I can't make that promise, Kat, but I can promise you I'll talk to your dad about it. I love spending time with you, too."

"Ka chew!" Katrina sneezed.

"You're not getting sick on me, are you?" Millicent Meanie's face came to mind, the woman berating Poppy for going out in the rain. *Silly thing to do and you'll get sick. I've got enough to do without having to wait on you hand and foot.* What if it was true? A sick feeling lodged in the pit of her stomach.

Katrina shook her head. "I don't think so. I feel fine. Just some sniffles."

"Good. Wouldn't want to give your daddy a reason to send me packing." Poppy laughed, chucking Katrina's chin teasingly. She had told Katrina she wanted to stay, and it was the truth. Being with Katrina and solely responsible for her care, it felt like having a daughter. A temporary one, but still a daughter. For the rest of the time she was in Lincoln, Poppy was determined to shower the little girl with love—and she'd honor her promise. She was not giving up on sticking around to do the job she'd been hired to do without a fight.

It was like having her own pretend family.

Not that she would ever tell Jordan. That would be the surest way to make him send her packing.

Poppy gazed lovingly at Katrina as she slept in the magical tent. Last night, Poppy was not ready to turn in for the night and stayed up long after the child had gone to bed. Not wanting to wake her, she slept in her own room again.

"Time to wake up, sleepyhead. Today's a school day, so you can't dawdle," Poppy said, crawling in next to her, intent on tickling her awake.

Katrina coughed, rolling over to face Poppy. "I don't feel so good," she rasped. *Oh, no. No. No. Please, Lord, don't let her be sick.*

Poppy reached out to feel her forehead. "I'm sorry. What hurts?" she asked. Katrina's brow was warm to the touch and Poppy's worst fears were confirmed. Katrina was sick and had a fever to boot.

"My throat hurts," Katrina whined, her eyes glassy as they filled with tears.

"I'll go find you something to make it feel better. And I need to take your temperature. It looks like school is out of the question." Poppy shook her head. This was disastrous. Did she take Katrina to the doctor or not?

Temperature first and medicine to bring down the fever. Bits of information trickled through her brain. 98.6 was normal. Maybe it was simply a low-grade fever and nothing to be overly concerned about. There was still hope. Crawling out of the tent, she went in search of medicine to help.

Poppy returned and took Katrina's temperature. 102.4. A high fever confirmed her worst fears. "Here, drink this. If it doesn't bring your fever down, I'll have to take you to the doctor."

"I want to talk to my daddy," Katrina sobbed.

"Sure thing, sweetheart." How would she explain this to Jordan? She should have never danced in the rain with Katrina. Millicent Meanie had been right. If only Poppy had listened.

Please Lord, help Katrina to get better. Lifting the cup to Katrina's lips, she helped her drink the grape liquid. "Try to get some more sleep and we'll let the medicine do its work. I'll try to reach your dad. He's out on a trail somewhere and may not have good cell service." They had not heard from him in two days, and no cell service would have been the only reason he had not called his daughter.

Unless he had been injured. Something she had not thought of and prayed it wasn't true.

For Jordan and Katrina's sake.

"Okay. Thanks, Poppy." Katrina's eyes drifted shut.

Poppy left the room and located her phone. She refused to believe he was injured, blaming the silence on the lack of cell towers wherever he was. But even if Jordan did not answer, she would leave him a message and have him call.

His phone rang, bouncing to voice mail. It was no more than she expected. Letting out a deep breath, she waited for his pre-recorded message to finish. "Hey, Jordan. It's me, Poppy. I, ummm...well, you see, it's Katrina. She's sick with a fever and wanted—" Her phone beeped and Poppy glanced at the screen to discover she had an incoming call—from Jordan.

"Hey, there. I saw you called. I've been out of touch and planned to call and talk to Katrina after school. Is everything okay?" Jordan asked, the worry in his voice crystal clear.

"Actually, no. Or it will be. I hope. Kat woke up sick this morning. She's got a fever."

"How high is it?" he asked, getting straight to the point.

"102.4."

"Did you give her some fever reducer medicine? It's in the cabinet to the left of the sink. What other symptoms does she have? We just delivered the cattle to the new pasture location and I can catch the first flight out instead of returning via the trail."

"Yes, to the medicine. Sore throat and mild cough. Some sneezing yesterday. And I don't think it's necessary for you to come home. I can handle this." Or she hoped she could. "Oh, she was asking to talk to you."

"Sounds like the flu. Maybe she picked it up at school last week. I really think I should come home. It sounds like Kitty Kat needs me." Jordan sounded weary. Poor man was doing all this to make things better for his daughter and home, and Poppy was stepping right into messing it up for him.

"Jordan, I've got this. It's not the first time I've dealt with illness." She had taken care of herself as a child for the most part, her nanny much preferring the soap operas than childcare.

"I'll take your word for it, seeing as I have no choice. I'm so glad you are there with her. She likes you a lot. I can tell." He would not be so glad she was there if learned the truth. Should she tell him now and get it over with? Maybe when he got home would be better.

"Thank you," Poppy said, feeling relieved she had time to fix this.

"Have you called the school to notify them of why she's absent? And the doctor's number is on the side of the refrigerator."

"I haven't called them, but I will. And I'm hoping we won't need the doctor, but thanks for the information."

"Can I talk to her now?" Jordan asked.

"Let me check. I'm hoping she's sleeping again and giving the medicine a chance to work." Poppy walked down the hall toward Katrina's room, stopping to peek inside. Sound asleep, just as she had expected. She moved back to the living room before speaking. "She's asleep. Will you be accessible for her to call you when she wakes up? I'm sure it would do a world of good for her."

"I will be. We're not set to head back toward home till the morning."

"Perfect. I'll keep you posted."

"Thanks again, Poppy," Jordan said, before hanging up the call.

Katrina was lucky to have a father like Jordan. A man who put his daughter first in every way. It was admirable he had been ready to drop everything and return home. Something her own parents had never done. The downside was if Jordan found out his daughter was sick because Poppy was a terrible nanny and let her play out in the rain, he would never forgive her. Her chances of sticking around and changing Jordan's mind about her would be zero. And the last thing she wanted was to face more condemnation from him or anyone else in town when they learned the truth.

Poppy called the school to let them know why Katrina was not coming today. She toyed with calling the doctor but held off. It would be better to wait and see how Katrina was feeling when she woke up and to see if the medicine was working.

Her phone rang, the screen flashing a number she did not recognize. "Hello," she answered.

"Good morning. This is Harriet—from next door. I wanted to make sure you would home straight away after school today before I stopped in."

"We will be. Katrina's sick and not going to school."

"Sick? What's wrong with her?" The woman's sharp voice rattled Poppy.

"It's possibly the flu. I've assured Jordan I have it under control and he doesn't need to come home." It was the truth and it was not as if Poppy didn't know a thing about sick children. Unfortunately, parents sent their sick kids to school all the time, not caring about infecting others and disrupting the flow of teaching.

"I see. Well, in that case, I think I'll skip today's visit. I don't want to get sick. I would hate to miss my ladies club meetings."

"That's fine. Everything is under control. We definitely don't want to inconvenience you." Good riddance. The woman reminded Poppy far too much of her nanny.

"Goodbye, then. I'll call tomorrow to see how she's doing. You do have the doctor's number, don't you?"

"I do. Thank you, and goodbye." She had rather the woman not come over or call, but that was Jordan's decision. She was not sure how Jordan tolerated her knowing she was trying to matchmake her daughter to him. *Unless he did not know.*

Men could be obtuse about matters of the heart. Or in this case, matters of marriage.

Poppy stopped to check on Katrina and felt her forehead, the child still sound asleep. She was relieved to feel the fever had come down and the medicine was doing its job. There was no reason to call the doctor—yet anyway.

She gathered up some food to take to the cat, knowing Katrina would be worried about Matilda. Crossing the yard, she entered the barn, and the cat came running up to her, rubbing her head against Poppy's legs. Matilda's motor box was running on full speed, her purrs loud and vibrating.

After dumping the can of food into the bowl, she picked up the water dish and took it to the outside spigot, rinsed it out, and refilled it. Back in the barn, she set the dish down and stroked the cat's back, loving the attention. Poppy stood and turned to leave, surprised to see another cat coming through the barn door she had left slightly ajar.

"Well, well, who do we have here?" she asked, taking a few tentative steps forward and then dropping to her knees gently, holding out her hand. "Here, kitty, kitty," she called out softly. The kitten stopped and watched her intently, unsure what to do next. With medium-length fur, her coloring was mostly white with some black and brown splotched in. Except for her face. One ear was entirely black, and half her face was black.

Poppy laughed, deciding the kitten looked like a pirate with a patch. "Here, kitty, kitty," she tried again, holding out her hand. The kitten inched closer, smelling her hand. She rubbed her nose against Poppy's hand, signaling her approval. "Good girl." Not that she knew if it was a boy or girl, but judging by her small size, it's the side Poppy landed on. "If Matilda doesn't leave you any food, don't worry. I'll be back with more. I wonder where you came from and if someone's looking for you. I'll have to mention you to Harriet. She knows everyone and all the gossip so if someone's looking for you, she'll know. I'm sure of it. Until then, you can stay right here."

She stood and made her way to the barn door, needing to get back to the house to check on Katrina. She had only been gone five minutes, but she'd hate for the child to wake up and her not be there when she called out. Poppy crossed the yard, stepped onto the porch, and pulled open the door, surprised when out of nowhere, the kitten ran inside ahead of her.

"Out, kitty. You can't stay in here. Not my rules, but you've got to go back to the barn." It was ridiculous that she was trying to reason with a kitten. Poppy tried to catch her, but each time the kitten shied away, staying out of reach.

Poppy gave up after the fifth try. "Guess I should feed you; you're looking quite thin and hungry." She opened another can of food, put it in a bowl, and set it down on the floor. The kitten stayed back, but only until Poppy moved away. Keeping constant vigil on Poppy, the kitten gulped down her food.

Poor thing. There was no way Poppy would corner the kitten and dump her back outside. She knew what it was like to be alone and unwanted, as she was convinced the cat was a stray, judging by the way she looked and how hungry she was.

"Gilda. You look like a Gilda." Establishing a name for the kitten made Poppy want to keep her, as if she were hers. She had always wanted a pet and this one was acting as though she'd chosen Poppy. Jordan would notapprove, but it's not like it mattered. She was not staying for long anyway, and when she left, she'd take Gilda with her. And in the meantime, when Jordan returned, she would take the kitten to the bunkhouse.

Surely, he would have no reason to object.

Chapter Eight

♥

Poppy put the cat in her room and closed the door behind her as she left. It had taken some coaxing, but the kitten finally let her pick her up. Holding the soft kitten close, she had fallen in love, irrevocably.

She would have to put together a makeshift cat box just in case the cat didn't want to go back outside. Jordan would simply have to deal with her decision, and since she was doing them both a favor by sticking around, she would make sure of it.

After leaving a message on Harriet's answering machine about the kitten, she headed for Katrina's room. It was a lucky break the woman was not home, but she did want the kitten to be able to find its way home—if she had one. If not, she was Poppy's to adopt, and the more she thought about it, the more she was convinced it was fate for the kitty to show up when she did.

Poppy needed Gilda as much as the kitten needed her.

Easing into Katrina's room, she watched as the little girl stirred. "Good afternoon, sweetheart," Poppy said, easing a few strands of hair off Katrina's face before pressing the back of her hand to the child's forehead.

"What time is it?" she asked, rubbing her eyes. "Did I miss breakfast?"

"You sure did. You must have needed the rest. And the good news is that your fever is under control, so no doctor for you, young lady," Poppy said, reassuring the child.

"That's a good thing. I don't like the doctor's office or the dentist's office. They're scary."

Poppy gave her a gentle smile. "They don't mean to be. It's their job to help you. Maybe next time you have to go, you picture them in pink tights and a tutu. That should help keep you relaxed and there's no way you could be afraid of them because they will look silly." It was something one of her teachers had told her to help conquer her fear of giving a speech in class.

"You always have such good ideas." Katrina smiled. "I'm hungry. Did my daddy call?"

"I talked to him earlier and he said he'll have cell service the rest of the day. I told him you'd be fine and that I'd take good care of you. He's eager to talk to you, so why don't you two talk while I fix you some soup and a sandwich?"

"I'd like that," Katrina said, sitting up.

Poppy hit redial on Jordan's number and he answered straight away. "Kat's wide awake and eager to talk with you. She's doing great and the fever is staying down."

"That's great news. Thanks for the update," Jordan said, his voice warm and sincere, the sound easing Poppy's fears a bit.

"You're welcome. Here she is." Poppy handed Katrina the phone. "I'll be back in a jiff."

Katrina nodded. "Hi, Daddy," she said, her face lighting up as she spoke.

Poppy left to make good on her promise for food. Chicken noodle soup and a peanut butter and jelly sandwich. Every kid's favorite, or so she assumed.

She put it all on a tray, including enough for herself, so the two of them could enjoy lunch together.

She tapped lightly on the open door, peering inside to make sure Katrina had finished talking with her dad. Poppy could only hope the subject of dancing in the rain had not come up, at least not yet. In a perfect world, she would be long gone before it did.

"Daddy said he's coming home by Friday and he's got a surprise for me. I like surprises."

"That sounds wonderful." If he was not racing home, Poppy could only assume her secret was safe.

"Being sick isn't so bad in a magical tent with my new best friend." Katrina reached for her sandwich and took a bite. "Mmm. My favorite," she tried to say, the words almost indecipherable.

"Chew, swallow, then talk." Poppy had heard the words a million times; now she understood why. Poppy had assumed it was because Millicent Meanie didn't want her to speak. *Children should be seen and not heard.* How could she not assume what she did, but hearing Katrina now, she also realized a person could hardly understand. Not to mention the unsightly appeal of partially chewed food showing.

Katrina nodded. "Daddy always tells me the same thing," she said after she had swallowed her food. At least they were not on polar opposite ends when it came to parenting skills. Not that Poppy was parenting. She was the nanny, and it would be better for her if she did not lose sight of the fact. *The temporary nanny.*

They ate lunch, telling each other stories. Before long, Katrina yawned.

"Sounds like it's time for you to take another nap. It's the best thing for you. I'll bring you in some more medicine that should hold you until this evening."

"It tastes good. I don't mind. Grape is my favorite. It tastes like a lollipop." Katrina nodded.

"Perfect. And after your nap, I've got a surprise for you," Poppy said, eager to share her new friend with Katrina.

"What is it?"

"If I tell you, it wouldn't be a surprise." She laughed. "But I will give you a hint," she added, unable to see the little girl's smile slip even for a second. "There will be three of us."

"Is Daddy coming home?" she asked eagerly. "No, wait. It can't be Daddy. He said Friday. *Hmmm*, I give up. Can I have another hint?"

"That was your one and only." Poppy grinned.

"Please? I promise I'll go to sleep if you tell me."

"I don't think you have much choice about falling asleep seeing as you can barely stay awake. But as always, I reckon I can give in and tell you. Or better yet, show you. But you must promise me, five minutes and not a second more."

"Deal," Katrina said, her smile ear to ear now that she had gotten her way. For a sick child, she certainly knew how to wrap Poppy 'round her pinky. Or, the truth was, she had had her wrapped since the moment Poppy had met her.

"I'll be right back." Poppy headed for her room. She found Gilda curled up on the bed next to her pillow. "Come here," she said, scooping up the kitten. "I have a special friend I want you to meet." She nuzzled the kitten next to her face, enjoying her soft fur.

Walking into Katrina's room, the girl's eyes grew wide when she spotted the kitten. "You have a cat?"

"A kitten. She sort of found me and followed me into the house." Poppy smiled, holding the kitten out for Katrina to touch.

"She looks like Matilda, only she's littler." Katrina touched the kitten gently, letting her fingers run the length of her body. "So soft and cuddly. Are you going to keep her?"

"If no one claims her, I am. I've never had a pet before, and Gilda will be perfect for me."

"Gilda and Matilda. They rhyme. I like it and I like the kitty."

"I hadn't thought of that, but you're right. I thought after your nap, the three of us could have a tea party right here in your magical tent. With real tea and honey for your throat."

"That sounds like fun. But Daddy won't like the kitten in the house. He tells me no every time I ask."

"The kitten can stay with me in the bunkhouse. I'll handle your daddy, don't you worry none. Now get some rest, honey. The sooner you fall asleep, the sooner you wake up and we can have a little get-well party." She kissed Katrina's forehead.

"Goodnight," Katrina said with a yawn. "Gilda is a wonderful surprise. You're so lucky." Her eyes drifted shut and Poppy backed out of the tent and left the room. It was tea party preparation time, and it was going to be the best ever if she had anything to do with it.

Tuesday morning dawned bright, the sunshine cascading through the window. Poppy had slept in her own room, the kitten curled up beside her. She slid out of bed and went to check on Katrina. The little girl had not even tried to push her bedtime when Poppy called a halt to their make-believe story time.

It was exhausting keeping up with a sick child, always wanting to make her feel better and keep her occupied so she did not dwell on not feeling well. Katrina was still sound asleep, and Poppy made her way to the kitchen. Mickey Mouse pancakes were in order. A special treat for a special young lady, one guaranteed to put a smile on her face.

The tea party had been a big hit, Gilda an even bigger hit. The kitten was playful and had no problem sharing some of the tea-party treats. She even chased after little wads of paper Katrina tossed to the end of her make-shift bed. Poppy had tried to convince Katrina to move back into her own bed, but the little girl was not having any of it. And, of course, Poppy gave in.

A knock on the door surprised her, seeing as it was only eight a.m. and she wasn't expecting anyone. Not even Harriet would arrive on her doorstep this early. She pulled open the door. "Hello. May I help you?" The two older women looked vaguely familiar, but she could not place them.

"Help us?" one woman said, a smile etched on her kindly face.

"We're here to help you, dearie," the second woman said.

"Help with what?" She could not imagine what they were talking about.

"With Katrina, of course. She is sick, right?"

Poppy bristled at the implication. "Well, yes. But I can take care of her." The guilt she carried toward her part in all this put her on the defensive.

"Nonsense. Taking care of a sick child when you're all alone isn't easy. We know Jordan's out of town and want to help. I'm Rosemary Winters, and this is Beatrice Smithey. We're from the First Christian Church."

Poppy's forehead scrunched as she considered what they were telling her. It explained why they were vaguely familiar. They had spoken to her and welcomed her to town the day before yesterday at church. "I'm really doing okay."

The woman shook her head. "Honey, let us help. That's what neighbors are for." They moved forward to come inside as if the answer 'no' was not an option.

"Harriet Collins from next door has been checking in on us." *For what it was worth.*

"Now we both know her kind of help doesn't get much done unless it benefits her," Rosemary said, grimacing slightly, but enough Poppy could not dismiss the woman's dislike of Jordan's neighbor.

"Why don't you let us clean the house? And if you want, you can take a walk or go to the store. We can stay with the child. Katrina's such a good girl," Beatrice offered.

They sounded sincere, which came as a shock to Poppy. They were kind to her on Sunday, but it would seem their kindness was genuine. A novelty in her world. It would be nice to take a walk, but she would not leave Katrina alone. At least, not until she had run it by Jordan for clearance. "Thank you so much. But how did you know she was sick?"

"Honey, this is a small town. Let's see, Bonnie, the woman you spoke at her school, told the principal and he told me, and I told Beatrice. Word will be all over town by midday, so don't be surprised if others drop in. Most likely with food." Their generosity was overwhelming for a child sick with the flu.

"Katrina's really okay," Poppy insisted. She had already messed up with Katrina once, and giving Jordan more reason to send her packing for incompetency simply wouldn't do.

"That's wonderful. But this is about more than her. It's neighbors helping neighbors. Besides, showing others love and kindness is a great way to bring joy to oneself. By letting us help, we're happier."

It was all so selfless, there was no way she could refuse. It would be downright rude. "I tell you what, I will accept your sweet offer, but I prefer to just relax a moment if you don't mind." She would not leave them alone until after she'd gotten clearance from Jordan or Harriet.

"That sounds lovely, dear. Has Katrina had her breakfast yet?" Rosemary asked.

"I was just about to put some pancakes on the griddle. Mickey Mouse pancakes," she clarified. "I thought it would brighten her morning."

"I can tell you're sweet on the child. And she was such a gem on Sunday. It must be the effect you have on her," Rosemary said, smiling.

"You're too kind. She's good-natured all on her own. That's not something I can take credit for. Jordan's done an amazing job raising a very special daughter."

"But it's her smile that was suddenly brighter, more like the Katrina of old, before her mother passed away, God rest her soul. I think you were responsible for it and that you've been such a blessing to Jordan and Katrina," Beatrice chimed in, moving further into the house, and putting her sweater over the back of the sofa.

"I'm only here temporarily. He's planning to hire someone else, someone more like the two of you." Poppy found herself going for honestly, curious what these two women would have to say about the issue.

"You mean older." Beatrice frowned.

"Jordan can be a bit thick-headed at times, and this is one of them. Man can't see what's right in front of his face," Rosemary added.

"And what's that?" Poppy dared to ask.

"You." The woman turned and walked away toward the kitchen, not giving Poppy a chance to respond.

"Don't mind her. She has a good eye for matchmaking people, and I get the idea she's settled on you and Jordan as a couple." Beatrice shot her a conspiratorial winked.

"Neither of us is looking for a relationship, so it's a moot point." Jordan Perry already had one great love and wasn't looking for another. He was almost perfect but could never be hers. Poppy, on the other hand, wanted to find someone of her own, who could love her and cherish her the way Jordan obviously had loved and cherished his own wife.

"Then you have nothing to worry about. Let Rosemary have her fun."

"Well, okay, then." It was an interesting perspective, and one Poppy could not argue with. If she was not in the market, it did not matter what anyone said or did to the contrary. But couldn't the same be said for other aspects of her life? Something she wanted to think about now that she had a little downtime. The first since Jordan had left on the cattle drive.

Chapter Nine

♥

FOR THE NEXT THREE days, ladies from the church stopped by to see if Poppy needed anything and brought food. It was almost over the top, but a far sight better than anything she was used to at some of the other places she had lived. Until she knew if she could trust the outward appearance of sincerity, she would keep up her guard and not let people get too close. That way they couldn't hurt her.

There was more food in the refrigerator than they could eat in a week, which meant little to no cooking, and plenty of downtime and lots of self-introspection. Lincoln was a quaint town, and it and the people were growing on her. All except Harriett. But then, the poor woman was trying to marry off her daughter to the wrong man, and Poppy could not help but feel sorry for her. Maybe the appeal of having her daughter get married and provide grandchildren all while living next door was simply too attractive of a package not to interfere. At least she was staying away while Katrina was sick, afraid to catch anything.

The idea of staying in Lincoln after Jordan hired someone else had merit. If she could find another job, that was. There was no way she could bank on Jordan keeping her around, especially not after the rain dance escapade and his daughter's subsequent illness.

Poppy could put out feelers at the elementary school and see if they needed a teacher or perhaps even a paid substitute. Anything to get her foot in the door and buy her some time to figure out what to next would be nice.

Jordan had vouched for the ladies from the church via text since his cell service was spotty at best. With their help, Katrina had the best of care. Of course, the little girl had been a wonderful patient, making it easy for everyone to want care for her. When Katrina woke up yesterday morning, it had been a relief to discover she was feeling well enough to get out of bed. She was also well enough for Poppy to put an end to the ladies' visits after thanking them all quite graciously for their help.

Poppy had wanted Katrina to go back to school today, but the little girl insisted she stay home—just in case her daddy got home. Of course, Poppy relented, giving in to her pleas and bright smile. Another day wouldn't matter, especially if it made Katrina happy. Besides, what would she learn in one day that she would not learn next week?

They spent most of the day playing games and reading stories. They were playing a game of Go Fish when a text notification sounded on Poppy's phone. She picked it up, surprised to see Jordan's name attached to it. "It's your daddy."

Poppy smiled at Katrina.

"Let me see what he has to say."

"Read it to me. Is he almost here?" she asked excitedly.

"*Home in time for dinner. How's Katrina?*" Poppy read the text out loud.

"*She's doing fine. Good enough for school, but I let it slide. She's excited to see you.*" she continued, typing and saying the words for Katrina's benefit.

"Tell him I love him," Katrina said, trying to peer at the screen and making it more difficult to type.

"Why don't you tell him tonight with a great big hug when he gets home?" It seemed awkward texting love messages to Jordan.

"Okay. I can't wait till he gets here."

Jordan's arrival would signal the beginning of the end of Poppy's stay at the Perry Farms, but she refused to let it spoil her mood or her time with Katrina.

They resumed playing the card game, laughing like two little kids when someone got their wish. It came as a surprise when her phone pinged another notification ten minutes later.

Jordan: I made reservations at the Cattle Corral steakhouse to celebrate coming home and Katrina's recovery. For the three of us. Okay?

He had included Poppy, something that set her heart to racing. Whether from nerves or anticipation, she wasn't sure.

"Who is it?" Katrina asked.

"Your dad. He wants to take us to dinner to celebrate coming home and your good health. You game?" Poppy knew the answer before she asked the question, but it was giving her time to get her own reaction under control.

Dinner. Like a family. Just not her own family, but it would have to do for now because she wasn't about to say no.

"Yippee! Tell him yes."

Poppy's own sentiment was echoed in Katrina's answer. She nodded and typed out the words to accept his offer.

Poppy: Yes. Sounds great.

Not wanting to think too much on it, she pressed send before she changed her mind. "Done."

"Yay. We should go find something pretty to wear," Katrina said, jumping down off the chair and grabbing her hand to pull her out of the kitchen and down the hall.

They stopped at Katrina's room first and picked out a dress together. "Do you want me to help you choose your dress?" Katrina asked.

"I don't have much to choose from. Why don't you get dressed and brush your hair and then when I've changed, I'll come back and work on braiding a couple of pigtails."

"I like that idea. You're the best, Poppy."

"Thank you, that's a sweet thing to say. I think you're the best, too." It was the truth. Two weeks with Katrina and she was hooked. Actually, it had only taken days, the little girl quite the charmer with her sunshine attitude.

"Do you mean it?" she asked, her eyes wide.

"I do." Poppy leaned forward to wrap Katrina in a hug. "I'll be right back."

In her own room, she went through her two suitcases, searching for just the right outfit. Picking a blue knee-length cotton dress, she slipped it on. There was nothing special about it, but it was what she called a serviceable dress—one she could wear anywhere and it worked. Adding a touch of color with a white beaded necklace and white sandals, she was ready in minutes.

She applied a touch of make-up and brushed her hair. Gazing at her reflection, she wished there were more she could do, but simple was all she had. Besides, vanity was unbecoming and it wasn't like this was a date. They were celebrating good things, even if those things were the very reason Poppy would be leaving soon.

After returning to help Katrina finish getting dressed, Poppy tried braiding her hair. A task made more difficult by the youthful excitement of Katrina eager to see her father again. Just as Poppy finished, the sound of a car door slamming alerted her Jordan had arrived.

"I'm home. Where's my Kitty Kat?" Jordan hollered seconds later.

"I'm right here, Daddy." Katrina went flying out of the room to meet her father.

Poppy followed, watching as Jordan scooped Katrina up in his arms and hugged her. "You look so pretty. Are you all dressed up for me?" he asked, a twinkle in his eyes as he gazed at Poppy.

"I am. Isn't Poppy beautiful, too? She dressed up for you, too," Katrina exclaimed.

Poppy felt her cheeks flush warm with embarrassment.

"She does look beautiful. I'm a lucky man to have two good-looking dinner dates," he teased. This carefree, joyful Jordan was not someone she was used to. Being gone, he had missed his daughter and it showed with the depth of feeling in his eyes as he hugged his little girl.

"I'll settle for dinner companion, if you don't mind. Thank you for the lovely invitation."

"Has she been this formal all week?" Jordan asked, tickling Katrina.

"Oh no, Daddy. We had so much fun," Katrina managed to answer in between bouts of giggling.

Jordan's eyes crinkled with merriment. "But you were sick."

"Not for all of it. And even when I was sick, we had some fun. Tell him, Poppy."

"Maybe you can tell me over dinner. I need to change clothes really quick if we are going to get to the restaurant by six."

"Okay, Daddy. Poppy and I will be right here waiting."

Jordan headed down the hall and out of sight, leaving Poppy a chance to settle the butterflies in her stomach, and taking deep breaths to calm her pounding heart. It made no sense he had this effect on her, other than the fact he was a really nice guy. Make that a really nice, good-looking guy.

Fiddlesticks.

Jordan held the door open at the steakhouse, allowing Katrina and Poppy to enter first. He checked in with the host and it was not long before they were escorted to their table.

Several people turned to watch their progress, many waving hellos to Jordan and his daughter. There were even a few of the ladies from church who waved at her, giving Poppy a case of the warm fuzzies. She did not dare trust in the friendships she'd formed this past week. It was always like waiting for the other shoe to drop with one foot already out the door, but everything seemed so real with them.

Poppy moved to sit at the seat with her back to the wall so she could people watch, a favorite pastime of hers. As she moved to pull back the chair, Jordan beat her to it, indicating for her to sit down. He sat across from her, giving Katrina a seat between them.

"Here are your menus, and the server will be right with you. Enjoy your meal," the host said.

"Thank you." Jordan took the paper menus from her hand and passed them around. The woman walked away, leaving them to make their selections while they waited.

"What's good?" Poppy asked.

"That's easy. Steak. Any steak. Best there is in the county, as far as I'm concerned. It's in the spices and flame broiling technique they use," Jordan said, his enthusiasm and opinion over the top. He would make a great spokesman for any advertisement, although his good looks would bring the ladies to the Cattle Corral in droves.

"That's quite a tall order to fill. Even with all the choice of places I get in the cities where I've lived, I can't say as I've ever been able to make that claim." It was true. The best of the best was available—the trick was finding it. Still, she had never made such a strong claim for any of the places she ate.

"Just goes to show you, the city doesn't have everything." Jordan shot her a wink.

Poppy laughed, nodding her head. "I'm starting to figure that out."

"What can I get, Daddy?" Katrina held up her kid's fun sheet. "Can I have something from the big people's menu?"

"Kitty Kat, you can have anything you want." He handed her his menu.

"Yippee." Katrina looked it over, managing to appear serious as she considered her choices. If it was Poppy's guess, the little girl wouldn't know half the words. "Can I have this one?" she asked, pointing at the one she had decided on.

"*Umm*, so maybe I need to amend the anything offer." Jordan chuckled.

"But why, Daddy? It says big, right here." She pointed to the word to prove her point. "I want big because I'm hungry."

Poppy grinned. It was probably one of the only words Katrina recognized, but she was staying out of this discussion.

"But that's adult size big, as in huge. Even I couldn't eat that one. It's this big," he said, using his hands to indicate the size of a plate.

"*Hmmm*, okay. So, what's smaller that I can eat?" Katrina asked, easily convinced her father was right.

"The sirloin looks yummy. And it comes in a six-ounce size which is probably plenty for a hungry little girl. Especially since it comes with your choice of potato or mac and cheese, vegetables, and a freshly baked bun."

"That's what I want. With the mac and cheese of course. And can I have a Shirley Temple?" she asked, a hopeful look in her eyes.

"Sure thing, Kitty Kat."

Jordan was so good with his daughter. Watching the closeness between them firsthand like this was inspiring. This was what she wanted for her life. Katrina was a lucky girl.

"And how about you, Poppy? What will you have?"

"I'd like the same thing Kat's having, right down to the mac and cheese." Katrina high-fived her, pleased with Poppy's choice.

"Does that mean a Shirley Temple, as well?"

"It's worth considering." She tapped the side of her mouth. "But I think I'll have a glass of iced tea if you don't mind."

"Sounds good."

The server approached, introduced herself, and Jordan proceeded to rattle off the entire order. Poppy was impressed he remembered. Quite the gentleman farmer, it would seem.

After the woman filled their water glasses and left, Jordan sat back in his chair, looking relaxed. "So, tell me about all the fun you had. I don't remember being sick as fun," he teased.

"The best fun was before I got sick. We took an adventure walk and built a magical tent. Wait till you see it, Daddy. It's the best ever and we really sleep in it. It has fairy
lights and stars and a moon."

Jordan nodded. "It sounds amazing, and I can't wait to see it."

"Oh, and we danced in the rain. That was so cool and so much fun. Wasn't it, Poppy?"

"Danced in the rain?" Jordan asked, looking at Poppy, one eyebrow slightly arched.

This was the moment she had been dreading. It would have been better served as a dessert instead of an appetizer. "It was warm outside, so we played in the rain," she said, trying to downplay the incident, but all the while knowing it would all come out.

Katrina was practically bouncing in her chair with excitement. "We did puddle jumping and played chase. My hair was dripping wet by the time we got inside. It was the best, wasn't it, Poppy?"

"It was loads of fun." It was also the reason Katrina got sick, and judging by Jordan's expression, the thought had crossed his mind. The guilt of Poppy's actions still hadn't lessened, and she feared Jordan's reaction when he learned the truth. It was time to face the pied-piper and pay her dues.

"Sounds it. Except then you got sick and missed school, so perhaps we should make that a one-time occurrence," Jordan countered, his voice calm and confident. He too, seemed to know the art of compromise.

"Oh, Daddy. You worry too much," Katrina said, rolling her eyes.

Poppy couldn't hold back the laughter, even though inside the dread of the moment had her stomach in knots. Her time of reckoning with Jordan would come soon enough. She had a feeling once Katrina was in bed, there be a more detailed discussion. He was not one to hash things out in front of his daughter.

Jordan ruffled her hair. "I'm just glad you're all better now."

"Yeppers. Oh, and Daddy, I want Poppy to stay with us. Forever. I don't want another nanny. She's perfect."

Jordan shook his head. "Well, Kitty Kat, sometimes you can't always have what you want."

That wasn't true this past week. Poppy had given Katrina everything she wanted—and then some.

"But it's my nanny, so I should get to choose," Katrina said stubbornly.

"I was going to tell you this later, but I guess I need to tell you now. I've already hired someone to replace Poppy." Jordan's words fell like a cloak of darkness on Poppy.

It was the last thing she had expected to hear the first night of Jordan's return, and the last thing she wanted to hear. Period. "This is rather sudden based on what you and I discussed before you left."

"I agree. It was actually rather lucky. Laura Weston is the great-aunt of one of the ranch hands I rode with. She's a real nanny and the family she was taking care of just moved to Europe. It was like it was meant to be. You'll like her, Kitty Kat. I promise." Jordan smiled at his daughter, fully expecting her to go along with whatever he decided.

"But I don't want anyone else." Katrina huffed, folding her arms in front of her chest and shooting daggers at her father.

"I'm glad you found someone more suitable to what you wanted," Poppy said. Truly this was the end of her time with the Perry's, but hopefully not Lincoln. That part remained to be seen.

"Poppy still hasn't had time to show me the pick-up game or play hide and go seek. And what about our magical tent? We built it for us. I don't want to share it with anyone else." Katrina was not falling in line with her father's plans easily. She hated to see the tension between them, but it was to be expected given the little girl's feelings for Poppy. A new nanny was always a risk.

"Laura won't be here for another week and a half. I was hoping you'd stay on till then, Poppy. That would give you time to do more special things with Katrina. By the sound of it, Poppy and fun are synonymous." Poppy couldn't decide if he meant it as a compliment, but either way, it was a week and a half more to get her life in order and spend time with Katrina, easing the inevitable transition.

Poppy nodded, reaching out to take Katrina's hand. "I'll stay till then, honey. And I might be staying in town even after that. I'm going to apply for a job at the elementary school. Then we can still see each other sometimes."

"Promise?" Katrina asked, grabbing onto the lifeline Poppy had tossed her.

"I can't promise I'll get the job, but I can promise I'll see you if I'm still in town." It was the truth, and the bright smile back on Katrina's face made the commitment worthwhile.

The rest of the evening was enjoyable. Jordan told tales of the cattle drive, making them laugh with some of his antics. Katrina, on the other hand, told her fair share of her own stories. As for Poppy, she listened and laughed. She couldn't remember the last time she'd been this relaxed or felt this much at peace. The only downside was knowing there was a limited amount of time left with her make-believe family.

By the time they arrived back at the house, Katrina was worn out, her yawns coming closer and closer together. Jordan picked her up and started down the hall.

"I want Poppy to tuck me in too, Daddy. And wait till you see my tent." She yawned again.

"I'm right behind you, sweetheart. I'm just going to drop my sweater off in the room."

Jordon nodded and smiled, seemingly not in the least concerned about his daughter's attachment to her.

Poppy entered her room and glanced around, looking for Gilda. Her suitcases lay open on the bed, clothes tossed around as she had picked out what to wear earlier. Gilda lay snuggled in her clothes, making herself right at home. Between the kitten and taking care of Katrina, she'd forgotten Jordan's insistence she stay in the bunkhouse when he was in residence. She would have to pack her things up and move them back tonight and take the cat with her. Right after she said good night to everyone.

She made her way back to Katrina's bedroom, pausing by the door to listen to Jordan reading his daughter a story. The man deserved a father-of-the-year award. Poppy stepped in the room, even more surprised to find them in the magical tent.

"Come lay down with us, Poppy," Katrina said, holding up her hand.

Poppy looked to Jordan, unsure how to answer.

His smile was all the green light she needed. She entered the tent and lay down next to Katrina. "Don't let me interrupt *The Princess and the Pea*. We need to know if she finally gets some sleep," Poppy teased, taking Katrina's hand in hers.

Jordan continued reading, not at all daunted by the fact Poppy had joined them. As for her, she would have been seriously tongue-tied had it been the other way around. "The end," he said, moving to kiss Katrina on the forehead. "Time to go to sleep, Kitty Kat."

"Yes, Daddy. I love you."

"I love you, too." Jordan started to rise, using care not to knock down the tent.

"Good night, sweetheart." Poppy leaned over to kiss her forehead, much the same way Jordan had done.

"Good night, Poppy. I love you." Three magical words that knocked hundreds of bricks from around the walls of her heart.

"I love you, too. Sweet dreams and I'll see you in the morning." She rose and followed Jordan out into the hall.

He pulled the door closed and turned to face her. "You've made quite an impression on my daughter. It almost makes me wish I hadn't found someone to replace you," he said, his eyes twinkling in the overhead lights.

"Almost isn't good enough. At the end of the day, I'm still a goner."

"True, but you did promise to stick around town and visit." Jordan stepped closer, one hand going to her chin as he tilted her head up slightly, gazing in her eyes with an intensity only previously hinted at. The same gaze that curled her toes and made her heart race.

"I did at that." Now, more than ever, she wanted to stay in Lincoln.

Jordan lowered his head slowly.

"Meow. Meow," Gilda cried, rubbing against her leg.

"What the—" Jordan stepped back, an astonished look on his face. "A cat? What's a cat doing in the house?"

"It's a long story. Meet Gilda. *My* cat," she said, emphasizing the word my in the hopes to calm him down. "It's a stray that followed me back from the barn and I decided to keep her when no one claimed the poor little thing."

"But this is my house. I didn't even let Katrina have a cat and now you have one? I'll never hear the end of it from her."

"It was only until you got home. I'm moving back to the bunkhouse house tonight, and I'm taking Gilda with me. Problem solved."

"If you say so. I'm exhausted from the trail ride, so I think I'll turn in for the evening."

"Good night, Jordan." Poppy picked up the Gilda and snuggled the kitten in her arms.

"Good night."

The kitten issue was solved, but that still left one other problem unsolved. The problem of Jordan's almost kiss that seemed destined to be the product of a changed mind and one that would never happen. "Gilda, you're a sweet kitty, but your timing is lousy."

Chapter Ten

♥

MONDAY MORNING CAME ALL too quick, and before Poppy knew it, Jordan was out in the fields to work and she had dropped Katrina off at school.

The weekend had sped by, the three of them settling back into a routine. Poppy had almost bowed out of going to church, but she had made friends with the women and couldn't help but want to press forward. If she was going to stick around town, it wouldn't hurt to have friends and friendship was a two-way street. As long as she didn't rely on them, it would all work out well.

Jordan had sat next to her, his nearness wreaking havoc with her emotions. The almost kiss was still fresh in her mind, much to her consternation. It had clearly been a moment of temporary insanity on his part, and something he had steered clear of since.

Poppy missed staying in the main cabin, the warmth and coziness of a family setting like a teaser of what was to come. At least, when she found the right man to marry and settle down with. Her own happily-ever-after.

Pushing aside all thoughts of the man and the missed kiss, she decided there was no time better than the present to move forward with her plans of trying to get a job. She parked the car and made her way to the administration office. A young woman sat behind a desk, talking on the phone. Poppy waited until she hung up before approaching.

"Good morning. How may I help you?" the woman asked, brushing her straight black hair off her face. She had a warm smile and kind eyes.

"Hi. I'm Poppy Delacorte, and I was wondering if you were hiring. I'm staying in the area temporarily but was thinking of staying in town if there were any jobs available."

"Are you an educator or looking for something in administration?"

"I'm a teacher—elementary school to be exact. I've taught kindergarten for the past four years." She left off the part it was at four different schools. Her resume would spell it out if she got that far in the process.

"That definitely qualifies you," the woman said, nodding her head as she pulled out an application packet. "I know we're looking for a second-grade teacher. We had one go out on maternity leave. Why don't you fill this out and I'll have Mr. Johnson look over it? He's the school principal and has final say so on all applications."

"That would be lovely. I can fill it out right now if you don't mind me sticking around. I'm free until two when the kindergarteners are finished for the day."

"Oh, do you have a child attending school here? I don't seem to recognize you." The woman tapped her fingers on the desk, her long nails striking the surface as she tried to place Poppy in her memory.

Poppy laughed. "I'm Katrina Perry's nanny. Temporarily, of course. Jordan has another woman who will be starting next Monday."

"Oh, that explains it." She nodded. "He's such a dreamy guy. How nice for you to be able to work with him. And Katrina is such a little darling." The woman's smile was firmly back in place.

"He's nice enough, but I couldn't agree more about Katrina." There was no way she would admit to anything else having experience the gossip chain far too often.

"Open your eyes and see what you're missing. Half the single ladies in town would give anything to become the next Mrs. Perry."

"I don't think he's looking, and I would consider myself in the other half—the not-looking group. I should get started on the application." There was no way she wanted to sit around and gossip about Jordan, especially when she was not exactly honest about her feelings toward the man. How could she not like him? He was perfect. Just not perfect for her because he was not looking for marriage and happily-ever-after, and Poppy wanted the dream. No matter how much she tried to deny it.

"Sounds good." The woman's phone rang, putting an end to their conversational opportunity.

Poppy sat down and filled out the application, glad she had her resume on her phone. With the way she moved around, keeping paper records would be impossible. An hour passed, the receptionist got up several times, making copies, getting coffee, and answering phones. She went into the principal's office several times, cast a glance in Poppy's direction, and then returned to her seat.

When Poppy finished, she made her way to the woman's desk. "Here you go. Thank you so much for your help. My phone is the best way to contact me if someone wants to talk to me."

The woman took the application from her. "That won't be necessary. Like I said, the teacher left a little earlier than planned on maternity leave and Mr. Johnston is eager to find someone. He'd like to talk with you now if you have a moment to spare."

A surprising twist, but then, in a small town, it would seem anything was possible. "That would be awesome. Thank you so much."

"Right this way then. My name's Debra." They shook hands and then Debra tapped lightly on the principal's door before opening it. "Poppy Delacorte turned in her application and I've got it and her right here for you, Jack."

"Thank you, Debra. Send her in."

Poppy followed Debra in, and she pointed to the chair in front of Mr. Johnston's desk. "Have a seat. Can I get you coffee or water?" she asked.

"Water would be nice, thank you." Poppy was nervous and having something to hold to would serve as a great way to calm her fidgeting and therefore all outward appearances of insecurity.

Debra handed Mr. Johnston her application and then left. Things were moving much faster than she expected, which worked well for Poppy.

"Thank you for sticking around to talk with me. Names Jack Johnston, but please, call me Jack." He came around the desk and shook her hand.

"It's nice to meet you."

"I can read your application, or you can simply tell me what I need to know." Jack was probably mid-fifties, his receding hairline and pepper-gray hair a giveaway.

"I can tell you about my experiences. Where would you like me to start?" This way, she would be able to gloss over the dates.

"Tell me what brings you to Lincoln and why you want to work here? And give me a little background on your teaching positions." The older man smiled, leaning back in his chair, giving her his full attention.

"That's easy enough to do." Poppy smiled. Ten minutes later, she'd covered all the important aspects of her teaching life and the joy she found in the job." *Without dates.*

"You sound perfect for the job. Providing all your references check out, of course. But tell me one thing—how did you end up in Lincoln as a nanny if you're a teacher?"

The not so easy question. *Please, Lord, help me to find the right words. The truth without the gory details.* Poppy took a swig of water, stalling for a few brief seconds. "Honestly, I broke up with a boyfriend, and the situation was uncomfortable, so I thought it best to leave. When I saw the advertisement in the paper, I thought it was a great opportunity to branch out and find another way to work with children. What I discovered though, was that teaching is so much easier than being a nanny." She grinned, trying to use humor as a way to get through this part.

Jack nodded, his fingers forming a teepee under his chin as he thought about her answer. "That's an interesting perspective. Why is that?"

"The children are here to learn. As a nanny, the battle between doing what's right and doing what's fun is a constant battle." It was the truth. She wanted Katrina to like her, to fit in, and she had gone way overboard trying to make it fun. Bending rules every chance she got. Not a good parenting skill by any stretch of the imagination.

"I love your refreshing honesty. Like I said, provided the references and background check all come back fine, is there any chance you could start Wednesday? Right now, we're rotating teachers into the classroom, and it's been a challenge at best. I think you are a Godsend to us."

It sounded very much like she had just been offered a job on the spot. It took her breath away, knowing what it meant. She did not have to leave Lincoln. Or Katrina. *Or Jordan.* Not that he counted in any real sense of being in her life. "Thank you so much for your vote of confidence. I would love to start Wednesday. I'll talk to Jordan to clear it with him, but since I'm only Katrina's nanny until next Monday, I'm sure he'll be okay with it."

"Wonderful. I'll be in touch tomorrow." Jack stood, shaking her hand, a broad smile on his face. They walked out of his office. "Debra, Poppy's going to start Wednesday if her all her checks come back clear. Can you pull the necessary reports and make some calls to expedite this process?"

"Absolutely. Welcome aboard, Poppy." Debra's huge smile echoed her words.

"Thank you, but it's not official until tomorrow."

"I'm not worried about the reference check and neither is Debra. She's the one who rushed your application to my attention. We're both good judges of character, so it's safe to say we'll see you Wednesday."

"Thank you both so much. I won't let you down. I've never taught second-graders, so I'll have to work on some lesson plans, but I'm a take-charge person and up to the challenge." She would make this work, no matter what.

Poppy left the school with a lighter step in her walk. Tonight, she would tell Jordan and Katrina. And tonight, it was her turn for a celebration dinner.

"Katrina, do you want to help me make dinner?" Poppy asked.

"I love to cook with you. I just wished you weren't leaving." Katrina's sad face was almost her undoing. She wanted to tell her about the new job, one that would have her at the same school as Katrina and where she could see her every day. But Poppy wanted this to be special. It was not often she had something to celebrate and people she wanted to celebrate with.

It was Poppy's very own type of magical moment. "Your daddy knows best. And I'm sure Laura will be just as fun and that you'll love her."

"But she's old." Katrina scrunched up her face, the idea not to her liking.

Poppy ruffled the little girl's hair. "Old can be fun, so don't let her age fool you. Promise me you'll give her a chance."

"I'll think about it," Katrina said, her voice way to serious for a five-year-old. "I don't want to promise something I can't do. I just want you, Poppy. I love you."

"I love you too, sweetheart. I promise you it will be okay." At least Poppy was keeping her own promise about staying in town and she would definitely visit. It would go a long way to keeping Katrina happy.

Maybe even enough to get her to give the new nanny a fair shot.

"What are we having?" Katrina asked as Poppy started pulling out ingredients.

"Cajun Chicken Pasta. One of my favorites. And for dessert, I thought we'd make a cake."

"What's Cajun?"

"It means a little spicy. Or a lot of spicy, depending on who's making it and who's eating it." Poppy laughed.

"So, which are we? A little or a lot?"

"A little spicy. I want you to like it because it's for a..." she stopped short, realizing she almost gave it away tonight was a celebration.

"For what?" Katrina asked, not missing a beat.

"For dinner. I want you to like your dinner," Poppy said, recovering quickly from the almost slip up.

"Well, if I don't, I can eat lots of cake. Chocolate cake is my favorite. Can we make that?"

"Sure thing, sweetheart. Anything for you." They were both chocoholics which made it easy to please the little girl.

Poppy pulled a stool over to the stove for Katrina. "I want you to stir everything gently as I add the ingredients. Think you can do that?"

"Of course, stirring is easy. Remember, I am five," she said, her matter-of-fact tone making Poppy laugh.

One by one, she added the ingredients, stopping on occasion to catch up the stirring process and to get the ingredients sticking to the edge of the pan that was missed in the stirring process. It was a recipe she had tested over and over, making small adjustments each time and was one she knew by heart. A few substitutions here and there would not hurt a thing, as Jordan's kitchen wasn't fully stocked with a wide variety of spices. She had picked up some smoked paprika at the store, knowing it was the one ingredient she wouldn't substitute for anything. It was a key ingredient that added smoke and spice to the creamy sauce, rendering the recipe perfect.

"Now we let it simmer and make the cake. Do you want to shower now or later?" Poppy asked.

"I'll shower now if you save me the bowl so I can lick the batter out." Katrina laughed. "Then we can play games tonight before my bedtime. I like games."

"Sounds like a plan." Poppy headed for the bathroom to turn the shower on and get it to the right temperature. "Holler for me if you need anything."

Poppy returned to the kitchen and mixed the cake, putting it in the oven to bake. She left the bowl with extra batter for better lickability. With that done, she went into the laundry room and sorted a load of clothes.

"I'm done and getting dressed," Katrina yelled.

Adding soap, she set the dials and took a load of Katrina's clean clothes to her room, putting them away in the drawers.

"Can I show you what I drew in school today?" Katrina asked, slipping into her pajamas.

"You sure can."

"Sit here." Katrina indicated the place next to her at the small desk in the corner. She pulled open her bookbag and took out several papers. This one I still need to finish by tomorrow, but this one I finished in class. Isn't it pretty?"

"It most certainly is. I love the way you mixed blue and pink in her hair. Very free-spirited." The color went well outside the lines, but Poppy only saw it as a reflection of Katrina's current artistic ability and therefore perfect.

"Tommy laughed at me. But what do boys know about girl's hair anyway?" Katrina scrunched her face in distaste.

Poppy nodded. "I agree. It's called imagination." It was one of the many things she loved about the little girl—her creative mind always in full-on mode.

"So, what colors should I use for the horsey in this picture?"

"Whatever you want. I've seen black, white, tan, brown, spotted. You get to choose."

"What about pink?" Katrina asked, a silly grin on her face.

"That I haven't seen, but I'm sensing it's your favorite color and you can color the horse any color you want. It's your drawing."

"My Little Pony is pink. Let me show you." Katrina slid off her chair and headed for her toybox. Digging down deep she searched for the toy. "Found it," she exclaimed. "See. Pink."

The sound of the alarm in the kitchen sounded through the house. "The cake," Poppy screeched. She raced down the hall to the kitchen, only to find it filled with smoke. She shut off the oven and opened all the doors and windows, hoping to clear the air.

"Is the cake okay?" Katrina asked, plugging her nose. "That's a lot of smoke." The nasally whine was funny, but now was not the time to laugh. No time would be a good time to laugh considering she'd ruined the celebration dessert.

"Ummm, I'm guessing the cake is a burnt disaster. I'm sorry." She did not want to open the oven door yet, wanting to clear the existing smoke out before adding more. Poppy flipped a towel in front of the alarm, waving it around, trying to get it turn off.

Once the ear-piercing shriek stopped, Poppy turned back to her pasta, only to discover it sticking to the bottom. Presumably burnt stuck.

The entire meal was ruined. Poppy's eyes watered as she fought back the sick feeling of failure.

"Are you crying?" Katrina asked, moving to stand next to her.

"No. It's the smoke bothering my eyes, sweetie. And I'm afraid our dinner is ruined. I'll have to find something else to make in a hurry. Your father will be home soon. Run along and do your coloring, and I'll clean up the mess."

"Okay. Are you sure you're not crying?" Katrina put an arm her, as though sensing Poppy wasn't as okay as she tried to make out to be.

"I'm sure, sweetie. Run along now," Poppy said, after a quick hug. Katrina was such a sweet child and not for the first time, Poppy wished she was her daughter.

Chapter Eleven

♥

T HE SMOKE HAD CLEARED but the odor remained as Poppy heated up some spaghetti sauce and noodles. It was almost six, and Jordan would be home soon. With any luck, he would be late tonight. She finished setting the table and went to check on Katrina.

"Everything okay in here?" she asked, spotting the little girl hard at work at her round table in the corner.

"Yeppers. Just finishing up. See," Katrina said, holding up her artwork.

"Very nice. I think the pink pony is perfect." Poppy grinned, enunciating the P words for added effect.

"Me too. I named her Petunia," Katrina added, crossing the room to hand the picture to her.

Poppy burst out laughing. "Great name."

Katrina tilted her head to one side, deep in thought. "What's so funny about Petunia?" she asked.

"Petunia, the pink pony is perfect. Get it?" Poppy said, once again stressing the letter P in each word, trying to help Katrina catch on to the humor of it all.

Katrina giggled. "Now I do. Wait till I tell Daddy."

"When you bring it back home from school, we can put it on the refrigerator." Not that Poppy would be there to make sure it happened. It was so easy to become embroiled in another life, making it harder to walk away from it when the time came.

Katrina's smile faded. "You have the bestus ideas, Poppy. I wish you wouldn't leave."

Poppy leaned down to give Katrina an encouraging hug. "It'll be fine, sweetheart. You'll see." Katrina would know just how fine tonight, even if Poppy had ruined the celebratory dessert. It was more proof she was not suited as a nanny, and that it was a good thing she'd taken the teacher's job.

Starting Wednesday, there would be less chances for mistakes. And by next Monday, nannying would be a thing of the past. Her failure also left her wondering about her hopes and dreams of one day becoming a mother. If she couldn't do this job, how could she become responsible for the life of a child who would depend on her for everything? "It's almost time for dinner. You should pick up your crayons and wash up."

"Yay. That mean's Daddy's almost home." Katrina placed her picture in her book bag, using care not to bend it. "Be right there."

Poppy headed for the kitchen, not daring to be gone for long after the earlier disaster. She had gotten caught up in the moment and spaced out everything else, which unfortunately was something that mattered.

She entered the kitchen and came to a halt, the sight of Jordan at the stove stirring the sauce catching her off-guard. "I didn't know you were home."

"Just got in. It smelled like something was burning so I thought I should check it out. But it seems just fine. Where's the smoke smell coming from?"

"I can explain. The smell, I'm sorry to say, is from earlier. We had a much nicer dinner and dessert planned but now, well, we don't. I guess I'm not as good of a cook as I thought I was." She winced, having to admit what happened to Jordan.

"Or a distracted one." He chuckled. "At least you didn't burn the house down."

She had expected his anger—but humor? Poppy had not seen it coming. "Thanks. There is that." It still did not make her feel any better about the whole fiasco. "It was meant to be a celebratory dinner," she admitted.

"And what are we celebrating?" he asked, pausing by the back door to remove his boots.

"I was offered a job at Katrina's school today. I'll be teaching second grade. Clearly, it's in the nick of time before I do burn your house down. I'm terrible as a nanny, cook, housekeeper. Don't know why I was thinking I could manage all this."

"I wouldn't agree," Jordan said, taking the plates out of her hand and setting the table for her.

"Oh, really? The fact is, I give in to everything she wants because I want to be her friend. I go overboard in everything I do. Like the dancing in the rain. I feel awful she got sick, and I know you haven't said anything about it to me yet, but it was obvious you weren't happy, and it wasn't a choice you would have made." There. She had said it. Got the elephant in the room finally exposed. It was better to clear the air all at once, taking a heaping dose of responsibility for her actions.

Jordan shrugged. "That's a fair statement, but it doesn't mean it was wrong. Just different. I like that you put Katrina first. It's all I could have hoped for in a nanny, even if you are a bit young to my liking." He shot her a wink before continuing to lay out the place settings.

How could the man tease at a time like this? "Age is always a physical thing. Maybe you should have considered me an old soul and given me a chance." If he could take a shot, so could she. Anything to eliminate the sick feeling of failure dancing around in her stomach.

"Maybe I should have, but there's nothing old soul about you. You love life and sometimes I wonder if you're trying to relive your childhood." Jordan's re-mark hit far too close to home.

"Quite the opposite," she said tentatively, wonder-ing exactly how much she was willing to reveal. Jor-dan made her want to tell him, a good indication she trusted him, something she did not do lightly.

"What's that supposed to mean?" He crossed the room to get the silverware while Poppy continued to stir the sauce, finding it easier to focus her attention on a mundane task than to face him.

"My childhood wasn't anything to write home about," Poppy said, forcing the words out. She was tired of living behind the cloak of secrecy and trying to handle the weight of her world on her own.

"Then how do you know so much about what kids want or would like?" He was trying to be nonchalant, but the intensity of his gaze proved otherwise.

"I had a nanny. The typical older, stick in the mud, walk straight, and fly right type of person. Children should be seen and not heard."

"Ouch. I get the picture and it's not very pretty." Doubtful. No one ever got the real picture. That image came complete with a red-letter T branded on her forehead for three days courtesy of unforgiving nanny. *Thief.* All she wanted was a small toy for her seventh birthday. It was wrong and she knew it and it was a mistake she never repeated. But if Millicent Meanie had her way, the keys to the prison would have been thrown away for life.

"Don't be. I'm over it." She shrugged, unwilling to reveal her darkest secret.

"What about your parents? Where are they?" he asked.

"Somewhere in Asia. *I think*. I get an occasional email updating me on their travels. They're botanists traveling the world in search of rare flowers." Saving the world one flower at a time.

Jordan shook his head. "I see. Was it always like this?"

"Yes. My parent's met in a poppy field in California while studying wildflowers. Hence my name. They married and then I came along, quite accidentally, of course. They traveled the world and let Millicent Beanie raise me in their absence. I nicknamed her Millicent Meanie." Poppy grinned. Using her own adaption of the woman's name had given her some small level of satisfaction that helped get Poppy through childhood. That and pretending all sorts of scenarios that made the woman disappear.

"I'm sorry. You've come a long way; good for you. And as to dancing in the rain, don't give it another thought. There are always germs at school, and there's no getting away from them entirely." "Thanks for being so understanding. My nanny wasn't. She told me I would get sick and under no circumstances could I go out and play in the rain. I did anyway, but I didn't get sick. She didn't appreciate me pointing out that fact and my punishment was doubled." One of many punishments over the years. The woman excelled at finding fault.

"Why didn't you ever tell your parents?"

"Because they were always running off on the next trip. I'd already been in their way just being born. I wasn't trying to make things worse. Besides, it's not like they would have believed me." Millicent made sure of it by putting on false airs and graces on the rare occasion her parents would stop at the house in between their trips.

"Sounds like a bad nanny. I don't think trading in for a new one would have been a bad thing.""You don't know the half of it. In hindsight, I should have. In hindsight, there's a lot of things in my life I wish I done differently. But you can't change the past, only the future." Poppy tilted the pan of noodles over the strainer to drain the water, careful to keep the steam away from her face and the water away from her fingers.

"That's a great attitude." Jordan came to stand next to her, reaching for the pan. "Let me help." His nearness sent her heart racing in double time. She let him take it, their hands touching in the process. Several seconds passed, neither saying a word.

Poppy let go, trying to recover from the moment.

Jordan stared at her intently. "I'm not sure I like the idea of you leaving us."

She sucked in a deep breath. What was he saying? "But you've got a nanny coming in and I've got to have a job. It's a win-win for both of us." She was trying to maintain a voice of reason, not wanting to fall down the rabbit hole of connecting dots that didn't exist.

"If I hadn't already hired the woman, I'm not sure I'd hire anyone. I've grown used to having you around, and I like coming home to you and Katrina. Call it selfish, but it's the truth." Jorden set the pan down on the counter and turned to face her. He leaned in, one hand sliding to the back of her neck as his mouth landed on hers. Gentle at first, and then deepening, her response matching his.

Heavenly. But not reality.

Poppy stepped away, breaking the kiss. After spending half her life trying to break free from her childhood and the other half with one foot out the door because of running from poor choices, she was not ready to trust anyone with her heart. Not yet.

Life is complicated enough without adding to it, and Jordan would be a complication. What else could he be? The man was still in love with his first wife. "I'm sorry. This isn't a good idea."

"What do you—"

"Hey, Daddy," Katrina said, skipping into the kitchen and hugging her father.

"Hey, Kitty Kat." He picked her up in his arms. "Did you have a good day at school?"

"I did. And wait till I show you my Petunia...umm, how did that go again?" Katrina asked looking at Poppy.

"Petunia, the pink pony who's perfect," Poppy answered, suddenly feeling carefree and lighthearted. The moment was over between her and Jordan, but it did not erase the joy in her heart.

Jordan chuckled. "That's quite a mouthful."

"Poppy says we can hang it on the refrigerator. That is if the new nanny lets me." Katrina frowned. "I'm sure it'll be fine, Kitty Kat."

"That's what Poppy keeps saying, but I'm not so sure. I don't want a new nanny, Daddy."

"Kitty Kat, the decisions have already been made." Jordan was staying strong in the light of his daughter's disapproval. He was a wonderful father, and the balancing act was not easy, but somehow, he managed to be both father and authoritarian. Katrina's love stayed strong even when she was unhappy.

Poppy kneeled, bringing herself level with Katrina. "Not only that, sweetheart, but I have some good news. I was going to share it tonight over dessert, but since there isn't any, I can tell you now. I'm going to be teaching second grade at your school."

"Really and truly?" Katrina asked, her eyes growing wide.

"Really and truly."

Katrina flung her arms around Poppy's next and squeezed, Poppy returning the sentiment of joy. "That's awesome. I can see you every day. But who will play tea party and go on adventure walks? Some old lady won't do that with me."

"If not, I'm sure there will be other fun things she'll do with you." Poppy did not believe it, and judging by Katrina's expression, neither did she.

Wednesday had been more than a little hectic trying to coordinate getting Katrina and herself ready. With each day that passed, Katrina grew more sullen. Poppy understood the fear of a new nanny, and it did not help that Poppy had spoiled her while she was there. Thursday had not been any better, and this morning, Katrina had a full-blown attitude problem. Unfortunately, Poppy did not know of anything that would make it better.

It would come down to Laura, the new nanny, and the impression she made on Katrina. Poppy prayed Laura would be kind and sweet, engaging Katrina on an interactive level that would help her grown into a strong young woman.

You only got to be a child once. Although in her case, Katrina had given her a chance to redo some of Poppy's. Jordan had been right in his assessment, not that she had admitted it to him. The kiss left them both a little wary around each other, both choosing not to discuss it or repeat the action.

The ride home from school had been an unusually quite one that had Poppy more than a little worried. Her attempts to draw Katrina into conversation failed miserably. Upon arriving at the cabin, Katrina had withdrawn to her room to do her homework. Granted it was coloring and fun, but it was still something she did not work on without prompting.

With dinner fixed and ready to go in the oven, and her lesson plans for tomorrow in order, Poppy headed down the hall to check on Katrina's progress. It was taking her a lot longer than usually and she had not even bothered to show up for her after school snack.

She knocked on Katrina's door before entering. Glancing around, she frowned. There was no sign of the girl in her room. Poppy headed for the bathroom but could not find her there either. A sense of unease traveled down her spine as she raced from room to room. "Katrina," she called out multiple times.

Poppy went outside and looked around. "Katrina," she called out again. Adrenaline surged through her when the little girl was nowhere to be found. She'd known she was upset, and it would seem leaving her alone wasn't the smartest of choices. Chalk another bad decision up to terrible nanny list.

She raced for the barn, hoping Katrina had taken the cat some food and was playing with Matilda. Except, she had not come into the kitchen. There was no sign of her, and Poppy feared the worst. What if she had run away?

It was something Poppy had considered many times as a child when life was going horribly wrong. She needed to call Jordan and did not relish the idea of admitting another failure. But finding Katrina was the most important thing right now. On the way back to the house, she pulled her phone from her pocket. Poppy veered toward the bunkhouse, just to rule out all the obvious places to look before she called him.

"Katrina," she called out, dashing around in search of Poppy, pulling open cupboard doors in the kitchen. Any place a child could hide.

Meow. Meow. Gilda was crying, but she had not greeted Poppy at the door as was her normal routine. "Here, Gilda. Here, kitty, kitty, kitty. Katrina, if you're in here, please come out. We can talk about what's going on. I'm sorry." It made sense if the kitten and Katrina were missing, they were most likely together. At least, Poppy prayed she was right.

Meow. Meow. The mews came from under Poppy's bed. She lay down on the floor, and sure enough, four eyes watched her as she inched nearer. "Thank goodness you're okay, Katrina. You had me worried out of my mind."

Katrina rubbed at her eyes and sniffed, the sight and sound breaking Poppy's heart. She had the kitten wrapped with one arm, holding her close. "Go away. You don't want to stay with me."

"I do, honey. But it's not that easy. Your daddy loves you and he's trying to do what's best. It's not like we won't see each other. I did promise to visit you." Poppy's heart was breaking for the sadness and tears on the little girl's face.

"But what if she's mean and rotten like your nanny?" Katrina sobbed.

Poppy paled. "What do you mean?" She had never told her about Millicent Meanie.

"I heard you tell Daddy about your nanny and how awful she was. I don't w-want...an old nanny. I w-want...you. Why can't...you s-stay here? Why d-does...it have to ch-change?" she asked, her voice breaking on every sentence.

"I'm sorry you overheard that part about my nanny. But she wasn't a nice woman, and your daddy wouldn't hire someone not nice. Plus, he's around almost every day and loves you very much. He'd never let anyone be mean to you." It was the truth, and somehow it was up to Poppy to convince Katrina and make this right. This situation was one more thing Jordan would not like. He probably could not wait to be rid of Poppy.

"*Hmmm.* I hadn't thought of that." Katrina rubbed her face with her free hand.

"Please come out and we can talk more. You haven't had your snack, which means neither have I. And we don't want to ruin our dinner."

"I am hungry." Katrina let go of Gilda who moseyed on up to Poppy, arching her back and looking for more attention. Inching her way out from under the bed, Katrina moved to sit next to her.

Feeling relieved, Poppy wrapped an arm around the little girl. "Let's go."

Arm in arm, they headed for the main cabin and straight to the kitchen. They would talk, and she would have to tell Jordan what happened, but she counted her blessings her discussion with him would not involve a search for his missing daughter. Jordan would forgive her a lot of things, but Poppy was not sure losing his daughter would be one of them.

By the time Jordan arrived home, Poppy was ready to face him with the truth of what happened. She should not have been spilling her guts to Jordan about her nanny. It was in the past and nothing was gained from digging in the past, and in this case it had proved damaging. *Lesson learned.*

Jordan came through the door, a tired and tense expression on his face. There was no way he already knew, so it must have been a bad day on the farm.

"Is everything okay," she asked.

Jordan shook his head. "Not really. We can talk about it later. After dinner." He rubbed the corded muscles at the back of his neck, casting a meaningful glance in Katrina's direction. "Hey, Kitty Kat. Did you have a good day?" Even on a bad day, he put his daughter's needs first.

Katrina glanced at Poppy and then back at her father. "Not really. I'm sorry I ran away, Daddy." Her eyes filled up with tears.

So much for not discussing serious matters until after dinner.

"What do you mean?" he asked his daughter, but his gaze was intent on Poppy.

"I can explain," Poppy said, trying to find the right words.

"Please do." The lines of tension had deepened on his face if that were possible.

"Katrina, can you give us a few moments? I'll call you when dinner's ready, but I want to explain things to your father." Poppy prayed she would do what was asked of her without a fuss.

"Does this mean I'm in trouble?" Katrina asked.

"No, Kat. You've done nothing wrong. This is my fault, so I'll do the explaining." There was no way she would let the child take any heat for this. It was all Poppy's doing.

"Okay." Katrina hugged Poppy and fled the kitchen, as if unsure whether her father would agree with the no-punishment-was-in-order theory.

"Start talking," he said, worry becoming more of a frown now with his daughter out of the room.

Poppy replayed the ride home from school, the homework, the missed snack, and ultimately her own search when she discovered Katrina missing. She was delaying the one part she did not want to repeat, knowing he would not like it, and knowing, it was also when they had both let their guards down and kissed. It would be a reminder of a moment best left forgotten.

"After I found her, we talked. I'm sorry, but it would seem it's my fault once again. She overheard me telling you about my nanny and assumed the worst about the new nanny since she's older."

Instead of being angry, Jordan almost looked, well—relieved. Which made no sense.

"I see. I'm glad she only went to the bunkhouse. She's a good girl and I can't imagine her going too far on her own. As to the other nanny and whether she'd be good or awful, it's a moot point now. I was going to wait until later to tell you this, but now seems like a better moment," he said, letting out a deep breath.

"What do you mean?" Poppy asked, amazed Jordan did not throw her out of the house instantly. Instead, it sounded like everything was okay.

"She canceled out on me. Her employer begged her to come to Europe and she's going. I have no idea what I'm going to do to replace her."

"Maybe I can help out a bit longer," she offered. "I've got to find a place to live and get settled, but while I'm looking it would be great if I could stay in the bunkhouse. There will be time I'll need to work on lessons plans and you'll have to put Katrina to bed, but if we can work together in the evenings, I think this could work well for both of us until you find someone else."

"Why, Miss Delacorte, I do believe you have yourself a deal. And Poppy, thank you. You're a life saver."

He wanted her to stay.

She wanted to stay.

Katrina wanted her to stay.

Temporarily, but still, it was more than she had when she woke up this morning. "I wouldn't go that far, but you're welcome, Mr. Perry." She winked. Katrina would be thrilled to have more time together.

Sometimes, the Lord's blessings came in mysterious ways.

Chapter Twelve

♥

SATURDAY MORNING, POPPY DROVE into town to pick up groceries for the week. She had not expected to still be staying at Perry Farms and had left the shopping to the new nanny. Having run into a couple of women she knew from the school, they were curious about the new nanny and wondering if she'd met the woman yet. Of course, the answer was no, which then elicited many more questions. Small towns had a history of knowing everything.

But there was one thing they didn't know, and she had no intention of telling anyone that Jordan had kissed her. Instead, she found a way to extricate herself from the conversations and hurried home. After putting away the groceries, she went in search of Katrina and Jordan.

"Hey there. Where's your dad? And are you up for an adventure walk again?" Poppy asked when she found Katrina coloring in her bedroom.

"He's in the barn. I'd love to go on another adventure walk. What will we be looking for today?" Katrina's voice grew excited as she started pulling on her shoes.

"What about birds? Maybe we can see how many we can identify while we are out and about."

"That sounds like fun, but you better do the writing. I'm not so good yet." She shrugged.

"You're doing just fine. It takes practice. I'll do the writing and let you watch as we sound out the spelling." It was an opportunity to teach and have fun, and she knew from experience it was almost every kid's preference. Children liked to try new things and it was all in the presentation.

"I'm ready, let's go." Hand in hand, they headed outside.

"Let's stop by the barn and let your daddy know what we're doing in case he comes looking for us," Poppy said.

"Good idea. I don't want to scare you or him ever again. I want to do what's right. And then maybe

Daddy will keep you here instead of finding me a new nanny." Katrina's chin rose a notch, the defiance in her voice on this subject still loud and clear.

"Your dad wants someone to live in the house to make things easier for him when he has to come and go throughout the day, or if he gets called away. It wouldn't look right if I stayed in the cabin and he was living there." Poppy tried to explain, hoping it would help the situation. Just saying "because I said so" was not working for Jordan.

"Why not?" she asked, the sweet innocence of childhood in the question.

Unfortunately, it was not something Poppy knew how to explain—but she'd try. "In the Bible, it says a man and a woman living together should be married. The church would frown on me living there since your dad and I are the same age and not married. It wouldn't look proper." Poppy hated that she was sounding more and more like her old nanny. Prim and proper—Millicent Meanie's favorite words.

"Then why don't you marry my daddy? You could live here forever." Katrina pleaded; her eyes wide with wonder as the idea took root. "And we could all live happily-ever-after."

Poppy chuckled. "It doesn't work that way, Kat. Two people should be in love. The reason your dad wants someone older is to make sure they stick around a while. Older women can be more settled." She was doing a hatchet job explaining it to Katrina and realized it would be better to change the subject. "Look, there's the first bird." She pointed to the barn gable where a bird had perched.

"What is it?" Katrina asked, momentarily distract-ed.

"That's a male cardinal. I can tell because of his coloring and size. Let's put it on our list." Katrina drew close and watched as she took out the pencil from her shirt pocket and started to write, sounding out each letter as she wrote it down. "Now, you read the letters back to me and tell me the word."

"C.A.R.D.I.N.A.L. Cardinal."

"Very good. And next to it, I'll add a note that says red male. This will help you identify them later."

Katrina nodded. "I like this learning game. I'll tell Daddy we're going on an adventure walk. Wait here, and I'll be right back." It was an odd request, but there was no accounting for the way a child thought things through sometimes.

"Run along then." Poppy watched as she ran in the barn and then turned her focus back to the birds, as Mrs. Cardinal had joined her mate.

Minutes later, Katrina came running out. "Daddy said it's fine. Let's go."

Poppy took her hand and they started down the path toward one of the unused pastures. She was hoping to see a wide array of feathered friends since this field bordered a wooded area. They spent the next hour and a half, walking and talking about birds, stopping to rest on occasion as Poppy jotted down more and more bird information. All in all, they had seen eight different kinds of birds Poppy could identify, and two she couldn't. She wondered if Jordan would have a bird book. It would be a great way to follow up their walk and to be able to show Katrina how to look up the ones they didn't recognize.

As they neared the house, Poppy was surprised to see Jordan talking to a woman. The two stood close, the woman's arm on Jordan's. The sudden pounding in her heart was closely followed by a moment of trepidation. Part of her wanted to stop and watch, part wanted to push the two further apart, but the biggest part of her reaction was centered on running away. She did not want to see Jordan with a girlfriend.

"Who's that?" Katrina asked, pointing at the woman with her father.

Too late to run away. "I don't know. Maybe your father has a girlfriend." It was wrong, but she had dangled the hint more as a way to see what Katrina would say.

"Daddy doesn't have a girlfriend. He says I'm his girl."

Poppy breathed a sigh of relief. "That you are."

"Hi, Daddy. We're back," Katrina said when they approached.

Jordan and the woman turned to face them, Jordan stepping away and putting distance between the couple. "Did you have fun?" he asked, picking Katrina up in his arms.

"We did. Wait till you see the list of birds we saw today," she said, her voice lit with animation. "Who are you?" Katrina asked, turning to the stranger.

"I'm Cecilia Dubois. And you must be Kat." The woman smiled, brushing her perfectly coiffured hair back with perfectly manicured fingers.

"Katrina. My name is Katrina Perry." Katrina had gone into an unusual defense mode with the woman, something Poppy didn't see happen often.

"Well, Katrina, I'm hoping your daddy will hire me as your new nanny. I think after meeting you, it would be a splendid idea." The woman brushed at something on her sleeve. If a little dust bothered her, she was hanging out in the wrong place coming here.

Katrina scowled. "You're too young. My daddy wants an old lady. Right, Daddy?"

"Well, Kitty Kat, it is certainly true about me wanting to hire someone older. I'm sorry you've come out all this way for nothing, Cecilia, but thanks for your kind offer," Jordan said, holding out his hand for a farewell shake.

It was the woman's cue to leave, an idea Poppy could not help but second, and she was positive Katrina would third.

Cecilia's smile faded. "If you change your mind, just call me. Here's my number." She handed him a business card and then slid back in her fancy sports car.

"I'm glad she's leaving. I didn't like her," Katrina said. Poppy agreed, but for very different reasons.

"That's not a nice thing to say, young lady," Jordan admonished.

"You always said to tell the truth. It's the truth."

Poppy hid her grin, not wanting to encourage the little girl down this path—but she did have a point.

"There's another part to that lesson we need to discuss. But tell me, why didn't you like her? You'd barely met her," he asked.

"She doesn't look like fun, and she's not at all like Poppy."

"Very true." Jordan nodded, setting Katrina down.

Poppy was not sure if his comment was an insult or a compliment, because from where she stood, the woman was put together perfectly in all the right places. Even her outfit spoke of class and refinement, something Poppy could not hope to achieve.

"Cecilia's not the first person to stop by since you left. It's been like a revolving driveway of young eligible women. I don't know how they know I'm looking for a nanny again, but the word is out. It's a disaster."

Jordan scowled; frustration evident in the tense set of his jaw.

Poppy and her big mouth. Was there anything she could get right? "Umm, I'm sorry. I ran into some women from the school, and I didn't realize it was secret information or I wouldn't have mentioned it in passing." She really did feel bad—for Jordan and Katrina.

"I see. Well, in a small town, or at least Lincoln, you tell one person, you've told the whole town within twenty-four hours."

"But it's only been a couple of hours," Poppy said, still somewhat astonished how fast the information had been transmitted.

"When anything happens that pertains to one of the town's bachelor's, and in a town where the ladies outnumber the men two to one, it's hot-off-the-press info." Jordan cracked a smile. It would seem he was letting her off the hook.

"I thought she was here for a job?" Poppy asked.

"The job of wife."

"Oh, Daddy. Remember what I told you," Katrina said, hands on her hips as she squared off with her father.

"Stop, Kitty Kat. Not going to happen. I've got you and you're all I need to make me happy." Jordan said, chucking her chin before he leaned over and kissed her forehead.

Katrina shot him an exasperated look. "You can be so difficult," she said, before storming off to run into the house, leaving Jordan standing there in shock.

"She'll be okay. It's a big adjustment for her and she has some definitive ideas of what she wants," Poppy said, trying to bridge the gap between father and daughter.

"You can say that again. Sometimes she acts like five going on twelve, and others, five going on two."

"She takes in everything she sees and hears and then regurgitates the information without a filter. She doesn't understand the half of what's going on. Everyone knows children do this so don't worry too much about it. There comes a time she'll have a good grasp of the language and then you'll long for the days when she didn't." Poppy chuckled.

"Well, for the rest of the day, since you're the one that started this madness, why don't you handle any unwanted visitors and I'll hide out in the barn."

"With pleasure," she said, except her reasons were not quite the same as Jordan's. For her, getting rid of the women hoping to catch his attention was like eliminating the competition for someone she did not even want to compete for. But judging by her earlier reaction, she was already starting to care for him more than she had planned.

The trick would be not letting Jordan know.

Jordan parked the car in the closest spot he could find to the church entrance, which still turned out to be in the back row. When he had asked her about going with them, Poppy agreed. It was an opportunity to see some of the ladies she'd met last week, having enjoyed their company as they chipped in to help her out with Katrina's care. Now that she was staying in town, Poppy was more willing to pursue their friendships, her normal reticence was quickly disappearing in the face of their extended kindness.

She had not known about the picnic afterward, but there'd been no turning back after Katrina found out. They entered through the big double doors and stepped into the large foyer. Several people stopped to talk to them, their warm welcome making her feel at home.

"Wait here and I'll drop Katrina off at children's church," Jordan said.

"Okay."

"See you after church, Poppy," Katrina said giving her a hug before moving off down the hall with her father.

Cecilia came to stand next to her. "Seems like you've established a comfortable position with Jordan. Coming to church like a family. Must be nice, but it leaves me to wonder why he wants to hire anyone else." There was an ice to the woman's voice that had not been there yesterday.

After Cecilia had left, there had only been two others Jordan had left Poppy to deal with, both far nicer than the catty woman beside her now. They just were not right for the position. "I wouldn't know. Maybe he likes having me around." She should not have said it, but the woman was sparking some of the anger Poppy felt toward the people in Whittling after they had denounced her without a fair hearing. Not that she needed to defend herself. People were too quick to judge in her opinion, which was their problem, not hers. As for her, she was better off without those kind of people in her life, and Cecilia was one of them.

"Maybe. Aren't you worried about your reputation?" The woman's eyes narrowed as she delivered her thinly veiled hint of impropriety.

Poppy was eager to be rid of Cecilia before Jordan returned. "Why should I? You weren't when you offered yourself for the position." It was the truth, but so typical of far too many people. Say one thing, do another.

Cecilia shook her head. "That was different. The people in town know I'm a good person. The same can't be said for you."

"Well, then we should let them make up their own minds. Have a nice morning." Poppy turned away, sending a direct message she was done listening to the nonsense.

"Oh, they will. Mark my words, they will." Cecilia's cold, no-nonsense tone slid over Poppy's skin, causing her shiver in worry, the threat all too real. Her comments evoked images of the past Poppy had run away from.

Trying to regroup, Poppy took several deep breaths. There was no way Cecilia knew anything about her or her past. It was a coincidence; she was simply speaking fighting words to let Poppy know she was not giving up on Jordan.

Jordan returned, a woman at his side. "Ah, there's Poppy. Please excuse me, we need to find our seats." He took Poppy's arm and led her inside, not bothering to wait for an answer.

"What was that all about?" Poppy asked, immediately calmed by Jordan's presence.

"Someone else applying for the nanny aka wife position. It's like I need to sky write *old women only need apply*," he teased.

"That's a thought." Poppy laughed. They took their seats just as the praise team began the music. Uplifting music filled the air, and Poppy basked in the warm glow as she sat there with Jordan, the words renewing her spirits after the run-in with Cecilia.

Jordan gazed at her several times, but remained silent, leaving Poppy to wonder what he was thinking. He made her nervous, the tension reminding her of something straight out of high school called first love. It was not possible and Poppy brushed the idea aside, focusing on the pastor's words of hope and truth, letting them soothe her soul.

An hour passed quickly, and soon, they picked Katrina up from the children's room and headed for the picnic area. The place was full of people already, giving the appearance half the town was present. Katrina and Poppy teamed up to play games, Jordan choosing to remain their own personal cheerleader.

Several women talked to him, some of who's flirty looks could not be misread. Jordan was not kidding about the women in town vying to come work for him.

Poppy, too, had her share of admirers. Men who wanted to get her something to drink, or ask her to take a walk, or her favorite—go to dinner tonight. Of course, she was not going to dinner alone with a stranger. Her replies had always been negative, none of which was prompted by Jordan's moody looks when he spotted her talking with someone. Correction, talking to an eligible guy. Served him right, because it was no different than Poppy herself had been feeling watching Jordan and the women. *Turnabout was a nice change.*

But it also made her realize she had come to care far more about him than she had realized.

"Is everyone ready to go home?" Jordan asked an hour later.

Katrina pouted. "But the picnic isn't over, Daddy."

"I've got some things I need to take care of, Kitty Kat. Maybe after, we can go fishing."

"You mean it?" Katrina brightened considerably.

"I do." Jordan ruffled her hair and picked her up, carrying her to the car. Poppy followed, not bothering to voice her opinion since, clearly, it did not matter what she wanted.

They rode home, the sound of Katrina's chatter the only real conversation as she told all about her morning in kid's church. When they arrived back at the farm, Katrina and Jordan headed for the main cabin and Poppy turned to the right, intent on retreating to the bunkhouse.

"Poppy, hang on a minute, will you?"

She paused, unsure what he could want. "Sure."

"Kitty Kat, do you mind going out to the barn and feeding your cat?" Poppy saw right through the comment. What he wanted to discuss clearly was not for tender ears.

"Will you come with me, Daddy?"

"I would but I need to talk to Poppy. Adult stuff."

"Okay," she said, shrugging. Katrina had only gone a few steps before she turned back. "Is this about what I told you earlier?" she asked, her eyes wide in wonder.

"Maybe, now run along," Jordan said firmly.

Katrina did a twirl. "Finally," she said, laughing out loud as she ran off toward the barn.

Poppy was more than a little curious. "What do you want to talk about?"

"Us. Katrina said something earlier today and at first, I dismissed her idea entirely. But then, I thought about it and her suggestion makes perfect sense."

There was no telling what this might entail considering it was coming from a five-year-old, but whatever it was, it had Jordan all wound up with tension. "Do I want to know?" she teased.

Jordan ran a hand through his hair and massaged the corded muscles at the back of his neck. "I hope so, anyway." He nodded. "She told me I should marry you and then you'd never have to leave."

"Marry me?" Nothing Jordan could have said would have surprised her more. She could not even begin to wrap her brain around his comment.

"Hear me out. You would get a place to stay, and I get a live-in nanny and housekeeper. Katrina gets a permanent female role model. You can still teach. It's a win-win solution, with the added benefit of putting an end to the single women vying for the position of wife." Put that way how could she say no? *Easily. This was nothing short of insanity.*

Poppy waited for him to reveal this was a joke, but he remained silent, waiting for her to speak. "This is so sudden. I can't for one minute believe you're serious, Jordan."

"Oh, but I am. Katrina loves you and I need you." His matter-of-fact voice sunk in, Poppy realizing he *was* serious.

She shook her head, trying to formulate the right words why this would not work. "I'm sorry, Jordan. I can't. I've always wanted love, marriage, and a family, but I want it to be real. I want marriage based on finding the right man God leads me to, not someone based on convenience. The answer is no. I'm sorry." It was nothing short of the truth and there had not been even the remotest hint of what she wanted in his offer.

"I see. Katrina will be disappointed, but it was worth a shot." There was no mention that he was disappointed, and there lie the bigger crux of Poppy's problem—she was the one to say no, but it had not come easily and it did not come without disappointment.

Chapter Thirteen

♥

Katrina had stayed after school today for a play rehearsal, giving Poppy some much needed time to catch up on things at the house. It wasn't often she had the place to herself, and she put on some music and settled in for a deep cleaning of the living room. Dusting baseboards and ceiling rafters, vacuuming under the sofa and chair, and some furniture polish and glass cleaner were all on her list of to-dos for the room.

Poppy stood on a chair, balancing herself carefully as she worked her way around the ceiling with a duster. George Strait music played on her phone app, Poppy occasionally unable to stop herself from belting out a few lines with her favorite country artist. Deep in the middle of "All My Exes Live in Texas," a different sound caught her off guard. She stopped dusting and looked around, shrugging it off when no other sound came.

Midway to resuming her dusting, the doorbell rang. She smiled. It was good to know she hadn't imagined hearing something that didn't exist. Climbing off the chair, she moved to the front door to open it.

Rupert Harris. Her ex was the last man she expected to show up here, and the last person she wanted to talk to. He stood there, looking all neat and polished in a suit, a cocky grin on his face. "Hello, darling."

Poppy made a move to shut the door. She had no idea how he found her, but she wanted him gone.

Rupert knocked again. "Come on, Poppy. We need to talk."

No we don't. She didn't bother to answer, just stood there, her back to the door as if to barricade him out of the house and her life.

"I know you can hear me and I'm not leaving until we talk. I've missed you." The snake hadn't lost his ability to lie, but he had lost the ability to charm her.

He wasn't playing fair, but then, when had he? Rupert was a first-class jerk, but unfortunately, Poppy believed him. And the last thing she wanted to do was to have him hanging around when Katrina and Jordan got home.

She pulled open the door. "Say what you have to say and leave," she demanded, arms crossed in front of her chest.

"Is that any way to treat me after I've come all this way to ask you to come home. You belong in Whittling—with me." Of all the arrogant men...this guy was the worst.

"I don't belong in Whittling anymore, thanks to you. And I definitely don't belong with you. After the stunt you pulled, I didn't dare show my face in town. Whittling's darling at his finest. How did you find me?" Not that it mattered, but she thought she'd done a good job covering her tracks.

"I talked to Mary Anderson at your old school, and she'd heard you'd applied for a job in Lincoln. And a blonde I met in town Saturday when I was checking out the area, was more than willing to share your whereabouts. Quite a looker and quite helpful." Rupert grinned, his gaze disconcerting.

It had to have been Cecilia, which explained her comment Sunday morning. "Well, unfind me," Poppy snapped.

"I can't do that. You know I love you. Your rejection upset me, and I acted poorly. I'm trying to make it up to you now. Come back, Poppy. I love you." The silver-tongue devil's lies rolled right off his tongue. Poppy wasn't about to fall for his tricks again. He'd ruined her life once. Never again.

"No. You're wasting your breath. You and I were never meant to be together. Go away, Rupert, and don't come back. You're not worth my time."

Jordan suddenly appeared out of nowhere and came up on the porch. "What's going on here?" he asked, his gaze darkening as it landed on Rupert.

"Nothing. Rupert was just leaving," she said, wondering how much of the conversation Jordan had heard. Maybe if she blinked, it would all go away and she could pretend it hadn't happened.

"Poppy's my girlfriend and I came to ask her to marry me. She's being stubborn and still mad at me because I rejected her like a fool when she wanted to take our relationship to the next level." The snake was still lying, his accusation in front of Jordan making her wish she could throw up, her stomach in knots.

The last time she had tried to defend herself against his lies, she'd come up on the losing end. It was not a route she wanted to travel again. "I'm being stubborn because we don't belong together. I've moved on. End of story."

"In that case, if the lady asked you to leave—you're leaving." Jordan took a step forward, a menacing scowl on his face. The last thing she wanted was for a brawl to break out between them. Rupert was not worth it.

Rupert looked back and forth between them, his expression darkening. "Are you staying with this man, Poppy? That's an interesting turn of events, don't you think?" She knew exactly what he meant, his true ugliness showing itself all over again.

"She's my nanny. Do you have a problem with that?" Jordan asked.

"Reckon not anymore. I love her. Loved her. Past tense. Any hope of reconciliation just died knowing what she's been up to behind closed doors. Nanny indeed. That's a good one. Guess I'm not good enough for her." This was exactly the scenario Jordan had tried to avoid when he had had her stay in the bunkhouse. Rupert's last comment was ludicrous, but Poppy had no inclination to correct him, only to have him leave.

Thank goodness Jordan was here to put an end to this. "Just go home, Rupert. It's over."

Jordan took another step toward him, his height more than a little intimidating.

Rupert turned and walked away, but she had seen the angry fire in his eyes. There was no telling what he would say about her in Whittling, but it was not like it mattered. She never intended to return there. Ever.

They both watched as he got in his Porsche and headed down the driveway, stirring up a dusty trail. "Thank—"

Jordan feasted an angry gaze on her. "What was that all about? The truth. Because from where I stand, it didn't sound so good."

He had come to her rescue but now she was not so sure it was a good thing. It was her life, and no explanations should be required. It's not like she asked Rupert to come here, and Jordan's attitude irritated her just enough to awaken her stubborn streak. "It's my private life and of no concern to you. I didn't ask him here. He's someone from my past who I choose to have no association with."

"Well, it sounds like he didn't have the same understanding." Jordan rubbed the back of his neck, lines of tension etched across his forehead. "I'm not sure you're the person I thought you were. It would seem you come with a past, and your resume certainly hadn't attested to some missing character qualities."

"Careful, Jordan. Passing judgement on what you don't know or understand is tricky business. No matter what you think of me, that doesn't justify that I should owe you an explanation."

"That's where you're wrong. Anything that concerns you at this point, concerns my daughter. Answer me this—I seem to remember you saying you wanted love and marriage, and yet a man shows up on my property claiming to love you. He also mentioned you didn't think he was good enough for you. Is that why you turned down my offer of marriage? A farmer isn't good enough either."

Poppy cringed. Jordan had it all wrong, but she was tired of fighting. "No, that's not why I turned you down. And you're wrong about Rupert and me, but you can believe whoever you want. That's what people do." There was no way she was going to tell him she was a virgin and saving herself for the man she loved, a man she had begun to think was him. Once again, her own judgement left a lot to be desired. "I think it's best if I left. Now."

She stepped off the porch and headed for the bunkhouse, not bothering to stick around for an answer. It would not take her long to pack her suitcases and then she would be gone. Katrina would be upset, but it was not like Poppy had a choice. At least she would be able to see her at school during the day, because Poppy would give a two-week notice and not leave the school in a lurch. They had put their faith in her and she would prove it was not misguided.

But when the people in town got wind of this, no one would pick her side, especially if Jordan had not. No one had believed her in Whittling, and she had be a fool to think Lincoln would be any different. At least this time, leaving would be of her own choosing. Call it running, call it cowardly, call it anything you want, there was no way she was sticking around.

Poppy wiped away the tears that persisted in falling as she packed her clothes. It was a good thing she had already picked up a cat carrier because she was not leaving the one thing that loved her without bias or judgement. Gilda and Poppy would move on.

For the next two weeks, she would stay at the motel in town, work out her notice at the school, and try to find another job and the next stop in her life.

Chapter Fourteen

♥

POPPY MADE A POINT of stopping by Katrina's home-room to give her a good morning hug and apologize for not being at the house. Katrina's tearful eyes had tugged at her heart, making Poppy second-guess her decision to leave. The only thing that kept her from changing her mind was the fact Jordan was trying to replace her anyway and it had only been a matter of time.

It was easier to make a clean break now.

Her second stop had been at the administrator's office to turn in her notice. Another meeting which had not gone well. They could not understand why she felt to need to leave, and she wasn't about to explain the dirty details. They would find out soon enough and be counting their blessings.

The day was long and drawn out, and by lunch she wished were back at the motel and napping. Not getting much sleep last night had not helped.

It was Poppy's turn on the monitor rotation, and she oversaw the children from the side of the cafeteria. So far, it was a good lunch period. No food fights, no rough housing, and no practical jokes. She glanced at her watch. Ten minutes to go.

Becky Thomas approached, her overpowering floral perfume proceeding her. "So, I hear there's more to you than meets the eye, little Miss Sunshine," she said in hushed tones, a fake smile plastered on her face.

Poppy stiffened. She'd never counted the woman as a friend, but this was the first direct confrontation, and it came as an attack Poppy hadn't expected. "I'm not sure what you mean."

"I heard about you. And so has most of the town, I'm almost sure of it. Trying to pull the wool over our eyes. Shame on you. And you claiming to be a Christian woman and all." Becky shook her head.

"I've done no such thing, regardless of what you think you heard." It was useless to defend herself, but she could not not make an attempt on her own behalf. There were two more weeks before she could leave and making them tolerable while she bided her time was a driving factor in how to proceed.

"Cecilia told me all about it. My sister had quite a conversation with the young man you seem to think you're too good for. Lucky for folks in Lincoln, the mayor's son is married already, or we'd have to warn him about you."

Cecilia's sister. That was something she had not known. Poppy pursed her lips, fighting the urge to responds. To open her mouth would be giving in to the temptation to vent her anger. Becky was just repeating what her sister had told her. Information that would-be all-over town by now if Becky was right.

"Rupert told her you wanted power and influence, and that your outer layer you showed the world was just a façade. Poor guy. You really hurt him with your scheming ways. You should be ashamed."

Poppy fought back her tears, the words like acid on her skin as they fell. Cecilia and her sister were mean-spirited women who feasted on weak people. If she showed any inkling she was about to beaten, they would torment her for the next two weeks—something she could not allow.

"You really should learn to get your facts straight. I've got to return to class, so why don't you stick around and look after the children for the next eight minutes." Poppy walked away, not bothering to wait for an answer.

"You can't leave. It's not my rotation," Becky huffed, calling out the challenge loud enough for some of the other teachers to hear.

There was no way she intended to stop or answer. Becky would have no choice but to stay the duration. Served her right.

Poppy stayed in the classroom for the remainder of the day, doing her best to engage the children and keep them focused on learning. Of course, extra reading time had been a blessing, but one that gave her too much time to think.

By the end of the school day, Poppy could not leave fast enough. Mostly, to avoid any chance of running into Jordan when he came to pick up Katrina. But also, to avoid any curious stares from other teachers. People like Becky and Cecilia would not stop repeating the gossip until they felt as though they were the reigning queens of information.

Instead of heading toward the room she had rented, she made her way to Main Street and headed for the church. The need for comfort and security overwhelmed her and she wanted to draw closer to God for the strength she would need in the coming days.

What she had not expected, however, was the curious stares along the way. People had heard. It was nothing less than she expected but facing them already had not been on her agenda. Coming here had been a miscalculation in judgment, and one she would pay for with a deepening of her already unstable emotions. Tears welled in her eyes as her body trembled, the pain in her chest increasing with each step and with each glance.

Honor would see her through working out the notice, but until it was over, she would keep to herself. No one wanted the truth or cared enough to ask her about. *Judging—always judging.*

Inside the church, Poppy found the solace and privacy she needed. Tears fell unchecked as she reached for a tissue, dabbing at her wet cheeks.

Father God, I pray you'll help me find the strength to see this through. Please forgive those who judge without knowing, as they've fallen prey to the evil lies spread by others. You know my heart, and the truth. I pray for peace and your guidance to help me find love and joy, Lord. In Jesus Almighty's name I pray. Amen.

An hour passed, and Poppy knew it was time to face the world once again. She could not stay hidden within the four walls of the church. She made her way to back of the church and into the foyer, pulled open the heavy door, and headed outside. The sunlight was blinding after the dim lighting in the sanctuary. Poppy shielded her eyes, reaching for the rail to guide her down the steps.

"Poppy?" a voice from behind her called out, grabbing her attention.

She tried to stop and turn at the same time, causing her to misstep. Her foot rolled to the side as she stumbled down the step, the sound of a bone snapping, followed by intense pain ricocheting from her ankle and up her leg as she landed on the ground. "Ouch," she cried out in anguish, reaching for her ankle. Her hands ached from where they contacted the concrete steps, a couple of scrapes reddening with blood.

"Are you okay?" a man asked, rushing toward her.

She looked up to discover the pastor kneeling to lend her assistance. "No," she cried out, unable to stop the tears from falling in a fresh wave. "I heard something snap. I don't think I can get up." Today had become the worst day of her life, or at least it seemed that way at this point. It could not get much worse.

"Sit tight. I'll call for an ambulance. I'm so sorry I startled you."

"It wasn't your fault. Please don't blame yourself. I should have stopped before I turned back." Another mistake and all her fault. When would she get life right?

The pastor made a quick call and was soon back by her side. "I was only trying to see if you wanted to talk about something. I was tied up in a meeting, but when I saw you leaving, I wanted to reach out. Is everything okay? I mean other than the obvious physical pain?" he asked.

"Honestly, no," Poppy said, tired of trying to put on a brave face. It was a heavy load to carry, and she'd do it alone, but there was no reason to shut out the pastor and his kindness.

"Do you want to talk about it? I mean, later, after your injuries been tended to," he asked, a gentle and concerned expression on his face.

"No but thank you. I learned a long time ago that talking won't change people or help the situation."

The pastor nodded. "No, but it can change you. Change your perspective and bring light."

"I'll think about it." The sounds of the ambulance coming down the street got louder as they pulled up in front of the church. They pulled up and a flurry of activity ensued as paramedics rushed to her side.

"What's going on," a young man asked, his gaze landing on her ankle.

"I tripped coming down the stairs. I heard something snap, so I'm pretty sure it's broken."

"Sorry to hear that." He said something into his walkie talkie and seconds later a gurney was pulled out of the back of the ambulance and carried to where she waited. "Anything else I should know about?"

"No. Just a few scrapes and a bruised ego ripe with embarrassment at being such a klutz."

"Accidents happen." The young man smiled. "We are going to be as gentle as we can be, but any movement is likely to hurt. I'm sorry in advance, but we need to get you on the bed. After that, we can keep you stabilized until we get you to the hospital and they administer some pain meds, get some x-rays, and then figure out what to do with you."

"Okay. Move away. I'm a big girl." She was used to pain, although not necessarily the physical kind. Poppy grimaced when they moved her, but she bit back any urge to cry out.

In less than fifteen minutes, she was settled into a room at the emergency center of the hospital in the next town over. It was not long before her pain was under control and the diagnosis reported. *Broken ankle.*

Something Poppy had already known. "I should have been a doctor," she announced.

"Doctor or no doctor, you'd still be laying right here."

"Oh, but then, if I was a man doctor, think of the all the nurses who'd want to help me." Poppy giggled. The pain relievers had kicked in but at the same time kicked out any common-sense filter on her mouth.

"I think if you were a woman doctor, there'd be plenty of men, nurses or otherwise, who'd want to help you." The doctor smiled at her, the teasing light in his eyes endearing. The man had to be in sixties.

"I doubt that. But I like your version of the story better," she quipped.

"Good. Now that we have that worked out, I'm going to give you a little something that will knock you out while we set your ankle in the correct position and cast it. You ready?"

Poppy pulled back, the doctors words troubling. "You're going to hit me? There must be a better way."

The doctor laughed and held up a mask. "Knock you out with anesthesia."

"Gotcha, doc. Do your worst. Or is that the best?" He placed the mask over her mouth and nose and before long she felt herself drifting off to sleep.

Poppy was grateful when Rosemary showed up at the hospital and offered to give her a ride to the motel. They had not talked much, Poppy preferring to sleep. When she woke up again, Rosemary was sitting in a chair, watching over her. The gesture of kindness was not lost on her.

"I see you're awake. You must be hungry," Rosemary said, rising and approaching the bed.

"I am, actually. I didn't eat breakfast or lunch." Poppy nodded. "Thank you for helping me today."

"You're welcome, dearie. That's what friends are for." Maybe so, but it was not something Poppy saw often, or trusted. It was also entirely possible Rosemary had not heard the rumors. The woman smiled, handing her a glass of water. "Here, drink this. You're probably thirsty as well from the anesthesia."

Poppy took a few sips, the cool liquid refreshing. "Thank you. I'm sure I'll be okay now, if you need to leave." Giving Rosemary an out was the easiest way not to deal with her condemnation later.

"Tsk. Tsk. Don't talk nonsense. Some of the others are on their way over with some dinner. Everyone wants to pitch in and help."

"Everyone?"

"Ladies from the church," Rosemary answered, not a trace of disproval in her expression.

It was only a matter of time before she heard the rumors. Before they all heard the rumors. "How will

I ever repay you?" Their kindness now would make losing them as friends all that much harder to bear. She had promised herself not to trust in friendships and yet, she'd clearly gone and done it anyway.

"Just be yourself."

"I don't know, that doesn't seem right." When the others arrived, they were sure to come carrying tales.

"Friends don't expect anything in return. It's all about the condition of the heart when a gift is given and received. And I know you've got a good heart." That confirmed what Poppy suspected; Rosemary had not heard the rumors. *Yet.*

A knock on the door had Rosemary moving to answer it. "Come in, come in. Our patient is just waking up."

"The poor dear." Poppy recognized Susan from church. The woman stepped around Rosemary and set her dish of food on the table and then crossed to the bedside. "The pastor blames himself for your accident and he feels terrible about the whole thing."

"It wasn't his fault," Poppy said.

"See, Susan. Pastor Mike is worrying for nothing. As for you, my dear, we're here to take care of you.

I'll fix you a plate of dinner. Susan's chicken pot pie is some of the best you'll ever eat."

"Thank you." Food sounded good, and well, chicken pot pie was one of her favorites. It was a comfort food and something she seemed to need frequently.

As she ate, two other women showed up, dropping off food and offering their sympathies and an outpouring of love. The small mini fridge was overflowing, and the table loaded with dish after dish of desserts.

It was the last thing Poppy expected, and though she was relishing their friendships, she had to know the truth, tired of waiting for the proverbial shoe to drop. "So, umm, I hate to bring this up. But it would seem none of you have heard what's going on with me, have you? I think it's only fair you should know what you're getting into when you associate with me." Warning them was the least she could do to repay their kindness.

"Associate with you? What nonsense are you talking about now, child?" Rosemary asked.

They all stopped and stared, waiting for her to answer.

"It's just that...well, you see..." Poppy was at a loss for words.

Sally, one of the newcomers to the group, slapped a hand to her head. "Good heavens, you're not talking about the silly rumors going around town today, are you?"

"Actually, yes." It was a relief not to have to explain.

"Goodness. Don't you know not to believe rumors?" Rachel said. Poppy struggled to keep all the names straight in what was turning out to be quite a large group in her small room.

Poppy was at a loss for words. *Not believe rumors.* Did that mean what she thought it meant or was it wishful thinking on her part? "I don't understand."

"We know you, and we're guessing what we heard is rumor. The definition of a rumor is unfounded information. Whereas we, on the other hand, are basing what we know about you on fact. We may be old, but we aren't blind," Rosemary said. "That counts for way more to the people who care about you."

Poppy scrunched her forehead in puzzlement, trying to keep up with the women. Whether the effect of the medicine, or the shock they knew and were still sitting here, she was not sure.

"Sweetie, don't let Cecilia or her sister get to you. They are not the pillars of our community, trust us." The women were genuine and caring, proof she had been wrong about them. It would seem she had finally found a community where she fit in, if only she didn't have to face Jordan. And if only she did not have to leave.

"Too bad Jordan doesn't see things the way you all do. Thank you for the vote of confidence. I really like all of you also, but unfortunately, I put in my notice yesterday. Staying in town isn't a good fit for me anymore."

"Why? There's no reason for you to leave town. If Jordan is upset with what he heard from the rumor mill, shame on him for believing it."

"He got his information firsthand." Poppy would not paint Jordan in the same brushstroke as Cecilia and Becky.

"But from who?" Rosemary asked.

"From Rupert, my ex. He just so happened to come to Lincoln, managing to destroy my reputation. Again." When would the nightmare end and Poppy could quit running?

"Well, there you have it. Just because your ex says it's true, doesn't mean it is. After all, he is your ex, and he's the man who came after you, and you're the one clearly still saying no. Tells me all I need to know."

"You need to stay put, dearie. Don't be running off again. It's high time you settled down," Rosemary said, taking her now empty plate away.

Poppy shrugged. "But Jordan..."

"Phooey on Jordan. He's just trying to protect his daughter. Anyone can see you're a good person, pure in heart and spirit. And mind you, men can be obtuse. Pay no attention to him. He's got a huge roadblock when it comes to Katrina and his own heart. Ever since his wife died, women have thrown themselves at him and he doesn't trust people easily. One day he'll wake up and see the error of his current path," Rosemary said, the other women nodding in agreement.

The women believed her. Believed in her. It was only Jordan who didn't. "He trusted me until Rupert landed in town spreading lies."

Rachel patted her arm. "Give him time, dearie. He'll get over it. You, running away, won't solve a thing. When you go back to school, you tell them you changed your mind and you're staying. Be strong."

Poppy nodded. "I'll think about it." It was a big decision and would require a leap of faith, something she had been in short supply of lately.

Everyone except Rosemary stood, gathering their belongings and saying their goodbyes. After they had gone, Rosemary came to stand by her bed. "They're right, you know."

Poppy wanted to believe them, but they did not know the whole truth. She trusted all the women, especially Rosemary. And she was tired of trying to do this on her own. "There's something you don't know, and I trust you won't repeat it, but maybe it will help you understand why I need to leave town."

Rosemary pulled up a chair and sat. "Go on, dear. I'm listening, and my lips are sealed." She dragged her fingers across her lips.

"Jordan asked me to marry him," Poppy said, plunging right into the meat of the matter.

Rosemary gasped. "What?"

Poppy nodded. "Yes. But it's not what you think. It wasn't love and roses and I can't live without you. It was a win/win situation proposal. He gets full-time care for Katrina and I get a roof over my head and a place to call home." His proposal still stung.

"What did you say?" The lines across Rosemary's forehead had deepened, but the woman was tiptoeing through the bomb Poppy had dropped.

"The only thing I could say—no. I want love. Is that selfish of me?"

Rosemary shook her head. "It was the right answer, and it's not selfish. Quite the opposite. Selfless. More proof of your inner beauty. Be patient, dearie. God will bring you someone special who will value all your admirable qualities when the time is right." She patted Poppy's hand to reinforce her words.

An overwhelming sadness rippled through Poppy. "At one point, I thought it might be Jordan, until he proved me wrong. His judgement of me wasn't based on fact, and I've had enough of that from other people throughout my life."

"I know Jordan quite well, and I can't imagine his offer of marriage was all based on a business deal. Have you considered at all that his reaction could be jealousy? I can't help but wonder if Jordan has feelings for you, and this is his way to escape something he's afraid of. Loving again." Rosemary had to be wrong. Jordan had never given her any indication he might care for her. Well, except for the kiss.

Poppy's fingertips automatically went to her lips. "I don't know, maybe. But I can't stick around and have my heart broken. I've been through too much."

"You were right to say no, dearie. If it's meant to be, it will happen in its own time. By not giving in to him without a full confession of feelings, I think he'll have to face his own fears and break through the wall around his heart. That, or risk losing you. He's a good man."

"I will think about what you said, I promise. I just don't know what to do, but I keep thinking leaving is best for everyone concerned. People in town won't be as understanding as you all were tonight." And she was tired of facing condemnation in everyone's eyes. She'd done nothing wrong and yet she was the one to pay a price.

"I think that's where you're wrong. Give them a chance, Poppy. No place is perfect, but you learn to sift out the bad and rejoice in the good."

"I'll try." She really wanted to stay. What if Rosemary was right? Could she stay if only a handful of people turned against her? And what of Jordan? His condemnation was the worst to have to bear.

Rosemary stood, sliding into her sweater. "I should let you get some sleep and give you some thinking time. Is there anything else you need tonight before I leave?"

Poppy shook her head. "I'm good. Thank you so much for your help and for listening. I promise I'll think about what you said."

"It's been a pleasure to help you. Your crutches are right here, and I'll be back in the morning."

"Thank you. I'll be all right, thanks to everyone who visited tonight. I can't remember the last time I felt the level of caring and warmth everyone showed me today."

Long after Rosemary left, Poppy thought about her words, and the words of the others. They were right, and it all boiled down to Poppy's confidence in herself to face the future, not knowing how it would all work out. Settling down and not running away was tempting.

More than tempting, because for the first time, Poppy felt as though she belonged somewhere.

Chapter Fifteen

♥

TRUE TO HER WORD, Rosemary arrived first thing in the morning. After an awkward and slow walk to the door as she adjusted to the large boot on her foot and crutches, she pulled open the door.

"Good morning, Poppy. It's lovely to see you up and moving. I brought breakfast so I hope you're hungry."

"Good morning to you, and yes, I'm famished. Thank you so much for doing this." Between managing the pain in her ankle and the pain in her heart, it had been a restless night. Rosemary's continued kindness was such a blessing.

"No problem. It gives me something fun and rewarding to do. How's the ankle?"

"I haven't been up and about much. Just a trip to the bathroom in the middle of the night and to answer the door for you, so it's hard to tell. The pain levels are still high, but at least I'm able to get around." One had to look for the positives when life was dealing you lemons all the way around.

"So true, and what a great attitude. It will carry you far in healing and in life. Why don't you hop back into bed and I'll fix your plate?"

Poppy moved to the bed, lowering herself carefully as she maneuvered into position, finding it easier to simply do what she was told rather than insist she could take care of herself. Rosemary pushed open curtains, letting the sunshine in the room, before moving to the table to open the bags she had put there. She pulled out a plate of food, added a few of the trimmings, and headed Poppy's way.

"Ta-da! Breakfast is served." Rosemary's bright smile lifted her spirits as much the warmth of the sunlight flooding the room.

"This looks yummy. I love sausage gravy on biscuits." Poppy topped it off with a little salt and pepper.

"This is the signature dish for our little diner in town, and they are known countrywide. Another blessing Lincoln has to offer. Have you thought about what I said last night, about staying?" Rosemary asked, not beating around the bush.

Poppy nodded, admiring the woman's directness. "I have." Somewhere in the wee hours of the morning she had come to a decision. Putting it into action would be more difficult, but it was the right thing to do. For her.

"And?" she prompted.

Saying what was in her heart would be like a commitment to herself, and tiny seeds of doubt held her back from announcing what she had decided. What if it was the wrong decision? How would she know? When would she know? Could she change her mind again?

She closed her eyes, trying to quell the doubts. *Be bold. Take control.* "I've decided to stay." Poppy said the words in a rush before she chickened out.

Rosemary smiled, letting out a sigh of relief. "That's wonderful, dear. The ladies will be thrilled. Please say you'll join our small group. We could use a youthful voice to help us branch out and find more ways to help folks around town."

Poppy was not sure she was ready for the commitment. "Thanks for the invitation. I'd love to join you but let me get back to work and get settled at a place to stay first." She did not want to be overwhelmed as she adjusted to the changes required in her life if she followed through with the decision.

"Well, the doctor said for you to take it easy for a couple of days before trying to do too much, but we don't want the school filling your position. Why don't you give Jack Johnston a call and tell him you've had a change of heart?" Rosemary was pushing her to take a leap of faith and jump in the deep end, eliminating any chance to change her mind.

It was also the push Poppy needed. "Sounds like a plan. I will right after I finish breakfast."

"Promise?"

Poppy nodded. "I promise."

"Good, I'm glad we got that settled. It's the right decision, trust me. Being brave isn't always easy, but in the end, the rewards can be magnified tenfold." Rosemary sat in a chair next to the bed.

"I'll bear that in mind with all the horrid looks I get from people in town that aren't as nice or accepting as you and the other ladies here last night," Poppy quipped, knowing the difficulties she faced.

"I reckon if you give folks a chance, they'll see the real you. I know your heart, dearie, and I believe that young man's assessment of you is nothing but lies. But do you want to tell me what happened? Maybe someone viewing it from a different perspective will help, and if nothing else it can set you free from the chains it's managed to wrap around you." Rosemary was like a mother, caring and always with a ready word of encouragement. Unlike Poppy's own mother.

Old habits of solitude and going it alone were hard to break. "It's in the past."

"But it's a past that still has the power to hurt you," Rosemary added gently.

It was true. "I used to date Rupert, the guy who showed up in town." Poppy told her the story in between bites of her breakfast, using the moments in between to gather her thoughts. "And so he showed up here, wanting me back. Of course, I said no. I'm not sure why he felt the need to come after me though. He'd already spread enough lies to make himself look better, so what was the point?" That was what really bothered her. Why follow her in the first place?

Rosemary shook her head. "You really don't see it?"

"No. What am I missing?" she asked.

"The way I see it, and I may be wrong, is that one of two things is going on. One, he really loved you and was missing you. He could be one of those of guys who is clueless how to act tough and be in love." Rosemary was giving Rupert a defense, but the tone of her voice said otherwise.

And Poppy agreed. "No, that can't be it. If he did, he could have never said anything bad about me and he most certainly wouldn't have spread lies. True love should stop someone from doing something to hurt the other person." Not that she was an expert on love, but she had read about it plenty in the hopes of understanding the heart and hoping when she found love she'd recognize it.

"Exactly. I was checking to see if you understood that, and to see how you felt about him and if you understood real love."

In some of the books, they referred to real love as an awareness that transcended the physical side of attraction. Poppy had experienced such feelings with Jordan even before he kissed her, but clearly, it was not love. Love was a two-way street for it to be real. "Well, I know what we had wasn't it, but I can't say as I felt real love before, so I'm not sure I totally understand it."

"Haven't you?" Rosemary grinned.

She was talking about Jordan. But Poppy was not ready to go down that road. No matter how much she thought it might be true for herself, would not make it true for them as a couple. "I don't think so," she said softly, not wanting to outright lie about something she did not fully understand. "What's your second theory?"

"In this scenario, Rupert isn't acting out of love. He put himself in the wronged and wounded warrior seat, looking for sympathy and to save face amongst his peers. To me, there's only one reason he'd show up here—some or a lot of the people didn't believe him. Now, he's trying to cover his tracks and find his way back to being the golden boy again in the eyes of the people around him." Her explanation was mind-boggling. And powerful.

"You really think so? I hadn't thought of that. But the people at the church, and our friends—"

"His friends, and perhaps the people closest to his family at your church. But a family doesn't own the congregation. Sooner or later, those that knew you would reveal the truth. Did you run away before giving them a chance?" Rosemary asked, pushing her spectacles back and staring intently at Poppy.

"Ummm…maybe. I hadn't thought of that. I ran, unable to face the haughty stares." She had run, finding it easier to believe the worst in people. It was something she had done all her life, Millicent Meanie's lessons affecting her every decision. All the more reason to dig in and stay in Lincoln.

"I, for one, am glad you left Whittling because it brought you to us. And to Jordan and Katrina. Sometimes, life has an interesting way of opening new doors."

"It brought me to Lincoln, for sure. The rest, not so much." Rosemary's wishful thinking would not make it true, but it was a sweet sentiment.

"Whatever God's plan for your life, make sure you're open and receptive to the message. You don't want to miss out on what's right in front of your face because you think you have it all figured out." Rosemary stood, leaning down to kiss Poppy's forehead. "I'm sorry, dear. But I've got to run. Make sure you call the school. You did promise."

"I will, and thanks again, for everything. And trust me, I don't have anything figured out, so I guess I'm good to go if I hear a message." Poppy laughed as Rosemary waved goodbye and walked out of the room.

Rosemary was determined to push Jordan in her direction, but the poor man did not want to be pushed or pulled for that matter. He wanted to stay in place—in the past. Poppy could not blame him. To have a great love for someone and then to be ripped apart far too early would be devastating.

Her heart wept for Jordan and Katrina's loss.

The relief in Jack Johnston's voice was all too obvious and filled with warmth and sincerity as he let Poppy know that of course, her position was still open. She would have missed the children she had bonded with, and now, it wasn't an issue. The more she thought about it, the stronger she felt that it had been the right decision. A bad decision would not feel this good, unlike the decision to leave had left her with a deep ache in her heart.

After promising to return to work on the next day, Poppy talked to the front desk manager about a place to live. He had given her several leads and she'd spent the rest of the morning calling around. With two appointments set for tomorrow, she lay down for a rest, the effort to get around exhausting and somewhat painful.

A couple of the women from church stopped by with more food and plenty of desserts. Rachel had just left when a knock sounded at the door again. Poppy hobbled to the door, wondering what she could have left behind.

"What did you forg—?" Nothing could have surprised her more than discovering it was Jordan and Katrina.

"Poppy!" Katrina exclaimed, stepping forward to hug her. It was awkward with the boot and cane she had graduated to using, but anything for this little sweetheart.

"Careful, Kitty Kat. We don't want her to have another accident or to hurt her any more than she has been already."

Jordan's gaze gave the words a deeper meaning, unless it was simply Poppy's heart playing a trick on her.

"She's okay. Sorry, I thought you were Rachel coming back for something. I wasn't expecting you." Poppy's heart raced uncontrollably, adrenaline coursing through her body having him in her room and without the tense scowl he worn in their last parting conversation.

"She left. We passed her in the hallway, but she said to ask you about the treats she dropped off," Katrina said, grinning as she looked around the room.

Poppy laughed. "Trust me, there's plenty of food for all. So many people have dropped off food, I can't begin to eat it all. Why don't you help yourself to the sweet treats and let me know what you find? I haven't had a chance to look everything over."

"Yay. I missed seeing you at school yesterday and today. I asked my teacher where you were, and she told me you got hurt. So, I wanted to come see you and cheer you up." Katrina moved to the table and was rifling through the various bags and opening each container to check out the contents.

"I missed you, too. And thank you for visiting. I'm trying to go back to work tomorrow, so I'll be sure to check in on you," Poppy said, knowing it would be good for both of them to have some sense of normalcy.

"That sounds awesome. Daddy, come look at all the goodies. Maybe there's something chocolate just for you."

"In a minute, Kitty Kat. Why don't you go ahead and pick something while I talk to Poppy for a second?"

"Sure thing," Katrina said, taking a plate and putting a few treats on it.

Poppy looked up at Jordan expectantly, wondering what he could possibly want to discuss. And for that matter, why he was here in the first place—unless it was for Katrina.

Jordan looked uneasy, running a hand through his hair before letting out a deep breath. "I came to apologize for what I said and how I acted. It was wrong. Please say you'll forgive me and come back to the house." So that was what this was about. He wanted her back—as a nanny. Each time she dared hope, he dashed it, and this time was no different. When would her heart learn?

"Thank you. Apology accepted." It was not as if she wanted to carry around a grudge; they were far too much weight around someone's neck, holding them back from life. Even Rupert, she realized. It was better to forgive and move him out of her life mentally and physically than to let his meanness continue to ruin her life or control her.

"That was easy. But then, you have a big heart. Something Katrina knows instinctively, but something I had to learn. Does this mean you'll come back to the house?"

This is the part where she had to stand firm. It was her life, and she was going to take control of it. Finally. "No. It's better that I don't. I'm sure you'll manage until you find a new nanny. It's nothing personal, but I've decided it's time to settle down, and I'm going to make Lincoln my home. I need to find a place to live and start over on my own. I've done nothing wrong, except trust people I shouldn't have, but now, I'm free of it all. Starting over. It's a wonderful feeling. And, of course, I'll still be able to see Kat and check up on her. It's what's best for everyone concerned."

Her words were a lie to what was in her heart, but it was the only answer she could give.

"I'm sure you will, and I understand. Maybe you're right. Otherwise, I might not ever let you go." Jordan's words set her heart to racing, making her long for something she could not have. She knew he did not mean them the way they came out, but then, he didn't know what Rosemary had figured out—she loved him.

Poppy nodded, trying to squash her runaway heart and feelings. "Thank you. Hopefully, I'll see you around town. And Jordan, thanks for bringing me to Lincoln, even if it was under a mistaken premise. I'd like to think Lincoln is where I was meant to be and that's why I'm here."

"I'm glad it all worked out." He nodded. It looked as though there was more he wanted to say but as Katrina approached, a shuttered expression crossed his face.

"I found a chocolate donut with sprinkles on top. Isn't it pretty, Daddy?" She held it up for his inspection. It had a large bite taken out already.

"It sure does, Kitty Kat. Good enough to eat," he said, leaning forward to take a bite.

"Silly Daddy, this is mine. There's more over there." She pointed at the table.

Jordan made his way to the table, surprising Poppy when he returned with two donuts and three cups of iced tea. "Can't have a tea party without everyone joining in." He handed out the cups and Poppy another of the delicious chocolate covered donuts.

"Thank you, don't mind if I do." Poppy grinned, more than okay with a little silliness.

"Yay, a tea party. Poppy loves tea parties, don't you, Poppy?" Katrina asked.

"I sure do, especially when it's with my favorite people," she said, taking a bite of the donut.

"Do you hear that, Daddy? We're her favorite people." Katrina beamed, chocolate icing decorating the corners of her mouth.

"I did hear. It was a super nice thing to say, so I should do a super nice thing and...wipe the chocolate off her face," he said, reaching up to brush the corner of her mouth. She thought he meant Katrina. The feel of his thumb as it grazed her skin, caused a new wave of awareness to flare into life with his tenderness. He cared, she already knew that, but that was where he drew the line.

And it is where she needed to draw the line.

"Thank you." She grinned. "And in turn, I'll take care of the chocolate on Kat's face." Poppy used the napkin to wipe at the corners of the little girl's mouth as she giggled. "I've got an appointment soon and wouldn't have wanted to embarrass myself, so thanks for the save, Jordan." Poppy was not sure how much longer she could keep her emotions at bay and needed them gone.

"Our cue to go, Kitty Kat. Drink up."

Katrina pouted. "Aww. I wish we could stay longer."

"I'll be back in school tomorrow and I'll see you then, Kat."

"Okay. See you." Katrina gave her a big hug, Jordan following suit. The two of them left, leaving Poppy to her privacy and her tears.

It was one thing to decide to stick around town and be brave, another to face Jordan and not let the sound of her breaking heart deafen her. She would be stronger and better, even face down Cecilia and Becky when the time came. But she was weak as a kitten when it came to Jordan and the sweet Katrina.

Chapter Sixteen

♥

TWO WEEKS FLEW BY between doctor's visits, house appointments, and school. It had not taken her long to settle on a small cottage to rent. The place suited her needs, keeping her in town and close enough to walk to the school, work, church, and the grocery store. Luckily, the ladies from the church had brought so much food, there was not much she needed, cutting down on trips to the store and agitation to her ankle. Outside of her time at school, she rested, preferring to read a book while sitting in the corner chair where the afternoon sun covered her with its warmth.

Each and every school day, Poppy made it a point to stop in and say good morning to Katrina in her classroom, and the two shared some conversations during recess when they happened to be on the playground at the same time. Katrina was a joy to talk with, full of stories from home. She was not trying to pry, but Katrina had been exuberant when she told Poppy that Jordan had ceased looking for a nanny and was handling things himself, spending more and more time with his daughter. Something Katrina was over the moon about.

The last few days she'd been more excited than a child on Christmas morning opening presents, but so far, Katrina hadn't said anything that would clue Poppy in to the cause.

Saturday morning arrived and Poppy was looking forward to spending the day fixing up her new place. With the decision to stay in Lincoln, her confidence in acquiring things had grown, buying things like decorations and a few pieces of furniture and having them delivered. They were furnishings she could not pack up in a suitcase and represented home. From the kitchen to the living room, to the bedroom and bathroom, she plotted and planned out her personal space. Most of the items continued to arrive all week, and she had been looking forward to today. Poppy was going to decorate her home space, marking it with a brand that declared it her home.

She unpacked the boxes, piling everything atop the coffee table and sofa she had delivered the second day after moving in. Walking with a cane slowed her down, but she managed to distribute the items in each room where they belonged.

A knock on the door prevented her from delivering the last of the cookware to the kitchen. Opening the door, she was happy to see Rosemary had come for a visit. "How nice of you to visit. Be careful, or I might put you to work." Poppy stepped back to let the woman enter.

"Good morning, dearie. Actually, I'm not here for a visit. Instead, I've come to collect you. I thought you'd enjoy a ride in the country this morning." The older woman's warm smile and kind invitation filled Poppy's heart with joy.

"That sounds lovely. One of these days, I'm going to have to break down and get a car so I can explore the area," Poppy exclaimed. She had had her heart set on decorating but spending time with people she cared about far outweighed something she could do in her free time. It was a far cry difference in her attitude with regards to forming relationships and learning to trust others.

"Well, for now, you have me. Your ride awaits."

"Let me grab my purse." Poppy retrieved her handbag, locked up the cottage, and the two were soon leaving Lincoln's town limits.

"How's the ankle?" Rosemary asked. It was the same thing she asked everyday she visited Poppy or called in to check on her.

Poppy shrugged. "Doing better. When I try to do too much it aches and reminds me to take it easy. The doc said six to eight weeks for the healing process."

"Well, I'm just glad it wasn't so bad you needed surgery. I can't imagine." Rosemary turned down an all too familiar road, sending Poppy's radar into overdrive.

"Me either. Where are we going?" she asked, frowning when Rosemary slowed and turned the driveway access to Perry Farms, confirming Poppy's suspicions. This was not on her agenda when it came to a nice drive in the country. Some things needed time and space, and her feelings for Jordan were one of them.

"I needed to stop here a minute on an errand, dear. I hope you don't mind." Rosemary glanced in her direction and then quickly looked away. Something was up, the older woman looking a little less sure of herself.

"Rosemary, what's going on?" Poppy was not buying her non-informational and all-too-convenient excuse of simply stopping by.

"It'll be fine. I want to show you something pretty special," Rosemary said, patting her arm. They pulled up at the house, passing a lot of cars parked on both sides of the gravel road.

"Can you give me hint? And why does it involve Jordan Perry?" She had been tricked into coming, but for what purpose she did not have a clue.

"You'll see." Short for Rosemary had no intention of telling her until she was ready for her to know. She parked the car near the front of the cabin and got out. "Come on, trust me."

"Fine. Lead away." Poppy got out, grabbing her cane and then followed Rosemary around to the side of the house, where a large crowd had gathered. "What's going on?" It took her a moment to realize it was a lot of people from town, but even more amazing was the newly planted field of yellow and orange poppies, resplendent with their full showy blooms. *California Poppies.* "This is incredible."

"The answers to your questions are right this way," Rosemary said, indicating she should keep walking. The crowd parted, reminding her of the passage in the Bible about the Red Sea parting. Except it was dry land on the other side. Jordan stood there, looking handsome as ever in blue jeans and a plaid dress shirt, his cowboy hat tipped to one side, giving him a roguish affect.

"What's going on, Jordan?" she asked, trying to put all the pieces together and coming up with nothing.

He closed the distance between them. "Someone once told me poppies grow better in California and I'm here to prove they grow the best in Lincoln, more specifically, right here on Perry Farms. You belong here, Poppy, and this field of poppies is for you. I want you to come back—to me and Katrina. We miss you more than you can imagine."

He was saying words she had longed to hear, all except the most important ones. There was no mention of love in his declaration. There was no way she could stay here and live with unrequited love. It would be her undoing after all the gains she made recently.

Be bold. Show confidence. "I don't know if I can, Jordan."

"What do you mean?" his voice cracked, matching the solemn look on his face. If she did not know any better, she'd swear he was heartbroken by her answer.

"Answer me this question. Is your offer to come back another marriage proposal?"

"It is," he said solemnly.

"Is the marriage offer for convenience because you need a nanny and a housekeeper or is for real?"

He reached for her hand and pressed it to his chest. "Real. That's what this is all about. I'm trying to show you how much I love you. I must not be doing a good job though," he said, a slight twitching grin suddenly appearing.

Her heart raced as he dropped the L word. "You're doing better than you think."

"I'm tired of running from the truth," Jordan said, moving closer so there no space left between them. In that moment, everyone else around ceased to exist.

"So am I." Poppy whispered the words, afraid to believe. "I think we've both been running from something bigger than each of us on our own."

"What's that?" he asked, love shining in his eyes. It was as real as real could get.

"Love. I love you, too. I have for quite some time but only realized it a few weeks ago. It's why I moved out and stayed away." Poppy dropped the cane and wrapped her arms around his neck, putting all her trust in Jordan. Her true love.

"You love me?" he asked, the joy in his expression like a light from God.

"I do. I just needed to put more faith in what I felt existed between us, but it's been so hard for me to trust. I've changed. I trust my heart and it's telling me I'm home. I've found where I belong—in Lincoln, and with you and Katrina. One question though, what's with the whole town being here?" she asked, casting a glance at all the people watching them.

"That's how the field got planted as quickly as I did. Plus, I wanted them to get the facts straight when I declared my love and proposed. First-hand information—and no rumor. So, will you marry me, Poppy Delacorte. Become my wife forever and ever?"

"Yes, I'll marry you."

Jordan kissed her right there in front of everyone. Loud cheers and clapping erupted as they shared in the joy of the moment.

Katrina ran up to hug her. "Does this mean you'll be my new mommy?" Katrina asked.

"Absolutely, my darling Kat."

Jordan picked his daughter up. "I think you should call me Kitty Kat then," she said, throwing her arms around Poppy's neck and pulling them all together for a family hug.

"All right then, Kitty Kat. I like it, and I love you."

"I love you too, Poppy."

Poppy pressed a light kiss to the little girl's cheek, her heart swelling with love. The sun came out, warming them all with the blessing of God. Faith had brought her love, home, and a family. All she had to do was wait on God's plan for her life to be revealed and to have trust everything would turn out exactly the way it should.

Epilogue

SIX MONTHS LATER...

The snow was coming down lightly, laying a fresh coat of white across the tree branches and ground. Angelically beautiful, the outdoor lights twinkling against their magic. Poppy gazed around, still in awe of how her special day had all come together, thanks to Jordan and his determination.

As an early wedding gift, he had located her parents and flown them to Lincoln for the event. Her parents had not been a big part of her life, but they were still her parents. And Poppy was thrilled to have her father walk her down the aisle. On the surface, it should not have meant so much to her, but it did.

They had come home to see her get married, and it was as if all the pieces of her life had fallen into place. They had never have a great relationship, but at least they had one. It was easier to forgive them and move on, knowing in her heart it was what God would want her to do. And in opening her heart, they had managed to have some fun over the past week of final preparations. And tonight, she had even claim her first father-daughter dance.

Maybe one day, they would even grow close. With God, anything was possible.

The outdoor wedding would be cold and quick, but inside the barn, Jordan had set up for the reception and the place was warm, with several of the neighbors pitching in with pot-bellied stoves. Twinkling lights and stars hung from the ceiling, with flowers everywhere. And of course, the centerpiece was made entirely of poppies that Jordan had flown in for the occasion.

They gathered together and stood before the pastor, hand in hand.

"Are you warm enough?" Jordan asked, his breath forming a frosty cloud as he spoke.

"I am. I still can't believe I let you talk me into an outdoor ceremony. We must have been crazy do this in the winter." She laughed.

"Crazy for you." Jordan dropped a kiss on her mouth. Every day was special with him because he went out of his way to make sure she knew it.

The guests were all snuggled warm in their winter coats, hats, and gloves. Poppy had not let vanity get in the way, and she too had on a white pea coat over her wedding dress. Time enough when they were inside for her groom to enjoy the lovely gown.

Katrina came to stand next to them. "Are we ready?" she asked, her eyes aglow with happiness. They were standing next to an evergreen tree, decorated with an odd assortment of ornaments. Jordan had insisted it was something he wanted to do, and it was the reason he kept insisting on having the wedding ceremony itself outside.

"It's my understanding you two wish to be wed in holy matrimony," the pastor asked.

"We do," they both said, eyes only for each other.

"It's my understanding that you each have written your own vows. Poppy nodded. "In the interest of the cold and snow, I promise to keep this short."

Everyone laughed.

"Jordan, you make my life complete. You and Katrina." She gazed lovingly at her new daughter. "From the beginning, you have been kind, generous with your family and home, and now your heart. I will cherish it forever. I love you."

"I love you, too. Sorry, folks, mine isn't as short." He chuckled.

Katrina handed him a microphone. Poppy had no idea what Jordan was up to, but knowing him the way she did, she knew it would be wonderful.

"As most of you know, when Regina died, I thought my ability to love died with her. Poppy brought my heart back to life, and I can only say I'm blessed to have the love of such a special woman. And with that in mind, I have a special song for her on this auspicious occasion of our marriage." With a twinkle in his eyes, he turned back to her. "On the first day of Christmas, my true love gave to me, a Poppy in a Pear tree."

Poppy shook her head and laughed, and so did everyone present. Jordan didn't stop there. He sang the entire song to her, pointing at the objects on the tree with each verse, and always pointing her as his Poppy.

It was the sweetest, most romantic thing she had ever heard. If she had not already been in love with him, this would have done the trick.

"Thank you all for playing along with my fun, but the truth is, Poppy is the love of my heart. It occurred to me that she would become Poppy Perry, and I couldn't resist." He looked at her and grinned.

Her new name was not something that had occurred to her, and it was funny. "I hadn't thought of that…maybe we should discuss this," she teased, not at all interested in keeping her maiden name.

"It's a mouthful for sure, but as luck would have it, Perry means pear as a family name, so the song stuck in my head and wouldn't let go. I love you, Poppy Perry," he said, leaning forward, his intent obvious to all.

"You may kiss the bride," the pastor said in a rush, making the kiss official.

"I now pronounce you husband and wife."

Everyone laughed and cheered as they hurried through the crowd, hand in hand, and led everyone inside the barn. The music started, and Poppy's father came to claim his dance. It was a magical moment for Poppy, but not nearly as magical as dancing with her new husband and daughter.

This was her new life. God's blessings were abundant and amazing, and He had led her right where she belonged.

***

What to read next?

If you enjoyed POPPY'S PATH TO LOVE, be sure to check out RACHEL'S ROAD TO LOVE in the GREAT SMOKY MOUNTAIN GETAWAYS series. And if you missed it, be sure to check out JULIET'S JOURNEY TO LOVE

BONUS READ

Want to keep in touch with new releases and what's happening in the world of Elsie Davis?

Sign up for the monthly newsletter at Elsie Davis HEA (Happily-Ever-After) and enjoy DIGGING THE DRIVER (A Celebrity Corgi Romance) as a FREE BOOK!

The greatest compliment you could give an author is to leave a review in order to help other readers discover the same great stories you enjoyed. Amazon/Bookbub/Goodreads are all great places. Many thanks!!!

Another great way to keep in touch - ***Follow Elsie Davis on FaceBook***

Also By Elsie Davis

Sweet, Clean and Wholesome Stories...with a Happily-Ever-After Guarantee!

Holidays in Hallbrook

(Sweet Romance Series for Holidays Throughout the Year)

Welcome to Hallbrook, New Hampshire. A small-town filled with the unexpected, lots of love, and of course, a beloved dog to ramp up the excitement.

Love & Order (Labor Day)

Love & Family (Thanksgiving)

Love & Peace (Christmas)

Love & Chocolate (Valentine's Day)

Love & Hope (Mother's Day)

Love & Liberty (Independence Day)

Love & Honor (Veteran's Day)
Love & Joy (Easter)
Love & Adventure (Father's Day)

Great Smoky Mountain Getaways
(Christian Inspirational – Women's Fiction Romances)
Juliet's Journey to Love
Poppy's Path to Love
Rachel's Road to Love

Crossroads Creek Cowboys
(Christian Inspirational Romances)
The Heart of a Cowboy
The Help of a Cowboy
The Return of a Cowboy
Coming Soon – The Care of a Cowboy

Crestfield Inn Romances
**If you like special kinds of soulmates, a splash of
the supernatural, and wholesome relationships,**

you'll adore this sweet bit of fun filled with romance and mystery.

Turning Back Time

Turning Up Roses

Turning Down Pie

Celebrity Corgi Romance

(Standalone Sweet Romance)

If you like light mystery mixed in with your happily-ever-after, you'll enjoy this second-chance romance and the race to save an adorable Corgi.

Digging the Driver

Gold Coast Retrievers

(Sweet Romance)

Special Golden Retrievers help their humans solve mysteries, save lives, and even find love...

Defending Dakota

Trinity River

(Sweet Western Romance)

Ranchers and farmers depend on the Trinity River for water, but when a secret conglomerate starts buying up property by fair means or foul, it's time for the landowners of Tumble County to fight back—Texas style. But what they don't count on, is finding love in the process.

Back in the Rancher's Arms
Small Town, Big Secrets

Coming Soon! (2023-2024)

Sundancer's Legacy – 9 Book series

Sundancer's Star
Sundancer's Joy
Sundancer's Heart
Sundancer's Majesty
Sundancer's Miracle
Sundancer's Glory
Sundancer's Kiss
Sundancer's Moon
Sundancer's Splendor

About The Author

Elsie Davis is a *USA Today and International Bestselling Author* of over 25 sweet, clean, and wholesome romances, and a member of the ACFW. She discovered the world of Happily-Ever-After romance at the age of twelve when she began avidly reading Barbara Cartland, the Queen of Romance, and has been hooked ever since. After building her dream log home on top of a small mountain, she turned her attention to do what she loves most, writing. Elsie writes sweet Contemporary Romance and Contemporary Christian Romance from her heart...hoping to share a little love in a big world.

When she's not writing, she can be found birding, kayaking, camping, fishing, playing disc golf, and taking nature walks—hoping to spot wildlife. Basically, she loves all things outdoors, EXCEPT cold weather. She and her husband are avid Caribbean cruisers, but Elsie's favorite vacation was their cruise to Alaska. (In spite of the cold!) Indoors, she enjoys a toasty fire, and of course, a great romance with a guaranteed Happily-Ever-After.

https://www.elsiedavishea.com